Critical Acclaim for Viken Berberian's *The Cyclist*

"Gorgeous line-by-line writing—rife with wordplay, punning, brutal lyricism, sensuous imagery, and spectacular rhyme. Reviewers will comment on Berberian's highly original prose style, readers and journalists alike are certain to arrive at the book for a decidedly more sensational reason: The novel explores the thoughts of a Middle Eastern suicide bomber during the days leading up to his final mission."

—*Poets & Writers*

"A surreal, intriguing novel . . . through Berberian's taut, sensual prose it is possible to see the world through a terrorist's eyes."

—*The Denver Post*

"The author's portrayal of the terrorist's psychology makes this stylish, troubling work a notable debut indeed."

—*The Dallas Morning News*

"An engaging, humorous first novel with a terrorism twist."

—*Tikkun*

"The novel holds the reader with psychological insight, with moral reflections that are not preachy."

—*The Buffalo News*

"Berberian takes us into fresh and disturbing territory."

—*The Toronto Sun*

"An arty, tantalizing little novel."

—*The Washington Times*

"Berberian is a thoughtful writer, delivering a compelling psychological portrait."

—Publishers Weekly

"Berberian has somehow—the somehow is actually highly skilled writing—managed to create a believable world in the mind of a young man about to end the lives of hundreds of innocents in what can no longer be called an unbelievable act. Deeply creepy and funny and perfectly timed."

—Kirkus

"Slim, precise . . . deeply literary, almost avant garde in style—[a] lyrical first novel."

—The Hartford Courant

The Cyclist

A Novel

Viken Berberian

SIMON & SCHUSTER

NEW YORK   LONDON   TORONTO   SYDNEY   SINGAPORE

SIMON & SCHUSTER
Rockefeller Center
1230 Avenue of the Americas
New York, NY 10020

First Simon & Schuster trade paperback edition 2003

SIMON & SCHUSTER and colophon are registered trademarks
of Simon & Schuster, Inc.

For information about special discounts for bulk purchases,
please contact Simon & Schuster Special Sales at
1-800-456-6798 or business@simonandschuster.com

Manufactured in the United States of America

10   9   8   7   6   5   4   3   2   1

The Library of Congress has cataloged the hardcover edition as follows:
Berberian, Viken.
    The cyclist : a novel / Viken Berberian.
        p.   cm.
    1. Terrorism—Fiction.   I.   Title.
PS3602.E75 C93   2002
813'.6—dc21   2001049339

ISNB   978-0-7432-4939-3

"The Diameter of the Bomb" by Yehuda Amichai originally appeared in *Poems of Jerusalem and Love Poems,* The
Sheep Meadow Press, Riverdale-on-Hudson, New York, 1988. Reprinted by permission.

    Excerpts from "The Just Man" and "A Season in Hell" by Arthur Rimbaud originally appeared in
Rimbaud: Complete Works, Selected Letters, The University of Chicago Press, 1966. Reprinted by permission.

For Hasmig and Levon

The atrocity that haunted the public execution played . . . a double role: it was the basis for a communication between crime and punishment, and also marked the exasperation of the punishment in relation to the crime. At one and the same time it demonstrated the splendor of truth and of power; it was the culmination of the ritual of investigation and the ceremony in which the sovereign triumphed. And both of these aspects were joined together in the body that was to be tortured and executed.

—*Michel Foucault*

The Diameter of the Bomb

The diameter of the bomb was thirty centimeters
and the diameter of its effective range about seven meters,
with four dead and eleven wounded.
And around these in a larger circle
of pain and time, two hospitals are scattered
and one graveyard. But the young woman
who was buried in the city she came from,
at a distance of more than a hundred kilometers,
enlarges the circle considerably,
and the solitary man mourning her death
at the distant shores of a country far across the sea
includes the entire world in the circle.
And I won't even mention the crying of orphans
that reaches up to the throne of God and
beyond, making
a circle with no end and no God.

—*Yehuda Amichai*

1

YOU SHOULD ALWAYS WEAR a helmet when riding a bicycle. The helmet should fit snugly. The chin strap should hold firmly against the throat. The buckle should be fastened securely. Consider this: last year there were 11 bike accidents in Iceland, 371 in France and 97 in England. I have no statistics from Holland, but surely, if I had been riding my bicycle on its flat land, I would have been spared my tragedy.

The same cannot be said about my place of origin. Nothing could have prepared me for it. Not even the helmet I took on my impossible tour from Mount Barouk to Beirut: a 71-kilometer calamitous road with a stretch of cedar trees on one side and flustered sheep on the other. There are few bicycles here. The main medium of movement remains the Mercedes 240D, with the runty Fiat coming in a close second. The cars cruise past the woolly sheep, with speeds in excess of an armored Hummer, their wheels rolling over steely lizards grilled in the heat of summer. No matter. I wanted this trip to be a trying hadj. In the West, you call it a pilgrimage.

I'll spare you the grisly details of my surgery, except to say that the butcher who sent me into my torpid sleep sliced a section of my gray matter like a knife-wielding chef about to serve a cold-cut platter. I now spend my days in a bed. My head is shaved. My limbs are sore and my face, which in normal times has a chocolate hue, is bludgeoned blue. My mouth smells like fermented lentil stew. My portly build has turned pita thin, the round bread I ate as a tubby kid. My diet is more severe than any I ever went on. I'm fed twenty-four hours a day, intravenously. In the morning, the nurse checks the tracheotomy. By noontime, the spectators flock in: sweet and sour faces from around the world; more friends, more family. A cauldron of compassion. It's the most unappetizing part of the day because they have no idea that in the hard prison of my head I can actually see them and hear everything they say. Little do they know that my typically lucid thoughts still race through my head with unparalleled speed, shifting into a lull only when I fall asleep. On the outside, I'm cool and composed: unable to swivel my neck or tongue, or, for that matter, any other part of my body. Not even my fiercely autonomous pinky. Yet every afternoon, when Ghaemi Basmati crawls into my room, my heart beats faster. Even before our calculated crime, our fates were intertwined like grapevines.

2

GHAEMI SNEAKS into my room with a tidy box of sweets. I hope that one day she'll cradle our baby too, softer than a puffy *choux*. My room smells like a hot oven tucked with tender loaves. Tempting treats in boxes of various sizes and shapes colonize the floor, some of them concealed under my sheets. "I brought you homemade matzo cake," Ghaemi says. My appetite is a mess. Even my unflappable eyelids lose their resilient steadiness. Ghaemi pokes her nose into my lumbering body, touches my face. She's hunting for clues, scouring my features to find traces of my robust cheeks: they're completely spent since my accident. I appreciate all the visitors who have flown from the far corners of the world to keep me company. If truth be told (with a teaspoon of refined white lie for flavor), they treat me as if I'm a cherub, pinching my cheek in an effort to make me squeak. Little do they know that a baby will remain in a state of stupor until it's ready to express its point of view. It takes time to simmer a bowl of Yemeni chicken stew.

I used to love Yemeni soup with atomic intensity. But my love for the dish burst like an embassy and I began to search for answers in cookbooks again. I borrowed them from my father's collection when he was out sipping black coffee with his highbrow friends. Many of the recipes he has acquired belong to a genre of fusion, sending the reader into complete confusion while undermining the tenets of the classical cook. My dad is something of an esthete, a wimpy art prof at the university. My ambition was to avoid the ranks of the literati. I dreamt of a less sedentary existence, convinced that truth cannot be found in text. That's why I'm salivating over my invitation to next month's event: a shower party that even the biggest superpowers of the world will be unable to prevent.

3

GHAEMI LIFTS MY ROBE and plucks my plums. She then slides her tortured tongue on my face. I'm concerned that my intravenous needle may fall out of place. Flavors can be very pleasing to the tongue at the start of a meal but fade with repetition, and while I am not in optimal physical condition, Ghaemi seems to think otherwise. "When will you come out of your sleep?" she asks. "The baby needs you. We're all counting on you." Like Persian rice stuffed in grape leaves, she rolls my penis in her palms. My glucose levels rise. My concentration of ions readjust. My mind drifts, and I begin to think about the shower party that I'm supposed to attend. This is the sort of shower party where the baby isn't really a baby and the gifts are wrapped in funeral colors like black and gray. It's the sort of shower party that will take place in a five-star hotel. Instead of pin the tail on the donkey, we'll spend the afternoon planting explosive mines in the hotel lobby. Instead of cheese blintzes, we'll munch on sabra: a regional cactus fruit that's thorny on the outside but soft on the inside, sort of like the denizens of this dusty place.

Ghaemi has never seen such an obedient subject. I'm a tantalizing tease: a splendid slice of Haloumi cheese. Except the doctors say that I have a lunar-like crater on the left side of my head. It's the part where they drilled an opening to reach my brain. But Ghaemi has no concept of pain. She steers a finger into my chest, and for a moment I cannot but help think that it's the rod of Aaron, which is an almond twig, pressing into me. The ancients attributed many wonderful virtues to almonds and so they ate them in great profusion, from peasant to king. When the almond trees blossom in white or pink (depending on whether they are bitter or sweet), they herald the hasty awakening of spring. Of course, some may prefer to see me in my current state—eternally motionless and in poor health—because in full bloom I am the incarnation of death.

Into the
Academy

1

MY BODY IS COVERED with bruises and bends, some of which precede the accident. The doctors have recorded seven so far. The largest is on my left leg, which is bent. There is one on my tummy and another on my troubled knee. The nurse uncovered one the other day, hiding somewhere under a mesh of hair. Little does she know that I acquired that one in London at the Underground Academy.

London was a sea change from my birthplace; above all it was a jolt to my sense of taste. Every Monday at noon they served flaky roast beef at the Academy's cafe, the Robinson Room. Mr. Robinson would have been gravely injured by the puddings we hurled, harder than a Gibraltar: you could not even chisel the damned rock with a silver spoon. As if the puddings were not enough, the porridge they poured from oppressive vats could make one swoon—in horror—

and not too soon. For a taste of the old country, I rode my bicycle to Edgware Road. I chewed on hot thyme bread and replenished my spices: sesame seed, saffron, powdered pepper and cloves. They made me forget this sour world. Many of the spice merchants came from abroad, the most dangerous from Aden and Doha. A sign in front of one of the grocery stores read: "From the Beeka to the Oriental Food Lover's Mecca."

"Will you attend the shower party?" whispers Ghaemi in my left ear. Feel free to nibble my left lobe, my dear. Sweeter than a dish fit for an emir.

Saddled with a heavy load, I spent broody afternoons trundling up Edgware Road. As I rode through London, my nostrils took in the smell of home: a mix of baklava and orange blossom. I'd ride past Halal Fried Chicken (HFC) and the Karachi Kafe, my stomach rumbling, my thighs working like pistons in splendid harmony. At the behest of the Academy, I rode my bicycle to the point of exhaustion. At the end of each day my legs would tremble and I would head back to the Academy in a drench of sweat. Sometimes Ghaemi would reward me with a baked noodle pudding called a *lukshen*. While I ate she took notes on how fast I rode. But that was not all. She would unstrap my helmet, measure my thighs and allow me an extra serving of the starchy noodles if I promised to ride a little slower the following day.

As a supplemental treat, Ghaemi would rub rosewater into her left armpit. "Why not the right?" I would ask. "I have always been predisposed to the Left," she would say. "It's part of my body politic, and I will practice it in every shape or form, until the struggle of our organized labor delivers humanity from the yoke of the enemy. Now finish your noodles. I want your nose in my left armpit. Inhale the good revolution."

Elizabethan women slept with apples in their armpits, then offered the fruit to their lovers for their olfactory enjoyment. For those who prefer ambient smells, there is always a pack of Kent. There is also the doctored trail of a perfume, which is more rotten than a tomb. None of these scents compare favorably to the vapors that emanate from Ghaemi. To smell her was to know the world. A whiff of her armpit could launch a jihad in the upper reaches of my nasal cavity. She teases my cilia, the whip-shaped molecular organs tucked in my nose, then lets them crack wild. My understanding of the chemical basis of our attraction is somewhat primitive. It seems electrical signals are produced when the odor molecule interacts with the receptor membrane. When the coding of signals from many cells are taken together, they lead to a collective explosion far beyond the nose, the convulsive consequences of which no hegemonic power will be able to oppose.

2

SOMETIMES EVENTS UNFOLD with the precision of a Mondrian painting. But there are other times when they look shifty, as in *trompe l'oeil,* an art term my father used at least twice a week, and an image is not always as it seems. From a distance I'm your average glutton. Come closer and my disposition worsens. I have been known to undergo many changes, and I often surface in random places. Like caramelized sugar, I have a talent for transformation. When table sugar is heated, it melts into a thick syrup, then slowly changes its color: from a light yellow it gradually deepens to a dark brown. As the sugar breaks down and recombines, it forms dozens of reactive offshoots, among them sour organic acids, bitter derivatives, volatile molecules and brown-colored polymers. It's a remarkable conversion and a fortunate one for the palate, although should my breakdown be followed by recovery, the by-products will prove to be more resonant. I was trained to yield a viscous batter, beating bodies liberally in a certain Near Eastern country, its territories and possessions, which may include, but are not limited to, attorneys and politicians, classical economists and central bank governors, military installations and preachers.

Owing to our historical position, it is the Academy's duty to oppose the forces of opposition. Updating the *Communist Manifesto,* our Designer of Deception, Sadji, once said: "We don't need to arouse the world's sympathy. We refuse to lose sight of our interests, to not indict the enemy in the interest of peace and security. Let the world know that it was *they* who first struck at us, violently, and whispered in our ears sinister prophecies of coming catastrophe. In this way arose the Academy: half lamentation, half lampoon; half echo of the past, half menace of the future; at times, by its bitter, witty and incisive criticism, striking them to the very heart's core; but always tragic in its effect through our belligerent capacity to comprehend the wild ride of modern history."

Under the Academy's strict orders, I surrendered to Sadji and his pack of riders. Struggling with my strokes, I could barely trail the cyclists. Yet my gluttonous build somehow served as a shield to conceal my true identity from the enemies of the Academy. In this respect, we were a vulnerable bunch, no different than a protein exposed to measured flame. When the heat is on, the protein molecule unfolds, exposing more of its atoms to reactive surroundings. The danger is that an agent such as heat can compromise the entire structure of a cell.

The Academy too believed that the world was a ripe threat, one we had to pluck quickly. So I kept on riding, pretending to escape my fate. I steered my bicycle into the unknown, trailing Sadji and gritting my teeth as he completed five loops around Hampstead Heath.

To tempt my zeal, the Academy invited me to a monthly food fest. Sadji would tell me in jest: "Help yourself a thousand times," as if not eating were a crime. It is said that when you feed friends, you buy their loyalty. Of course, that depends upon what kind of food you serve. You will never see me salivate over a tureen of lentil stew. But I could kill for a serving of *harissa,* cause grave bodily harm for a tart tabbouleh. Sadji spent considerable sums for his recruitment fairs. To my dismay, much of the food was continental fare. The dishes ranged from smoky garlic sausage with kale to grilled tenderloin with chanterelles. I am not sure why some people think that terror is so pernicious. Of course, when one's tummy is indulged, few things seem insidious. All I did was eat and ride whenever he did. I will never forget those days: it's easier to remember those whose bread we shared.

Outside these festive events, Sadji sank his stained teeth into grotty pub grub. Waving a frothy stout in his hand, he would tell me to never ride my bicycle fast. Easy enough, I thought, with a bag of wispy fries. Once he whisked to Milan's fashion Mecca, the tony Quadrilatero d'Oro, on a two-day crisis holiday with funds from our cash-strapped treasury. He came back sporting a £503 Dries van Noten blazer, which he preferred over English brands like Burberry. Fashion, Sadji used to say, is at its most serious when you don't even notice it: another appropriate lesson from a Gucci revolutionary. Fortunately, the dress code at next month's shower party will be decidedly low-key. Of course, the hotel's top brass may take issue with the ski masks we plan to wear. But that should be the least of their worries. Once they meet our unruly baby, they'll wish they were in hell. Their minutes shall be numbered, their children orphaned, their wives widowed, marching to a funeral knell.

3

WHEN I JOINED THE ACADEMY, my dimensions were as big as a de Kooning canvas. With the exception of Sadji, no one made fun of my weight. Ghaemi praised my prodigious body for its multilayered complexity. And the Academy was quick to look beyond my size. Six months into my training, I entered the inner sanctum of the Academy: an elite team called the Attorneys of the Shower Party. The Attorneys are four members with little training in law. We belong to a philosophical school, the origins of which are existential chaos. Ghaemi's bailiwick is bombs; mine is cycling. Sadji's is deception; Leng's is cooking. When I ate one of his date cookies, Leng would tell me: "The righteous shall flourish like the palm tree." The Academy is our home away from home, a place that nurtures our childhood affections with a gourmand's confections before posting us back to the ancient lands where we grew up, crowded with minarets, spires and domes.

4

I NEVER IMAGINED that I would be back in the Bekáa, swaddled and inert like a mummy, unable to move a grain of barley in my tummy. I am no longer a glutton. In fact, if it weren't for Ghaemi's secret visits I would be more gaunt than a desert Bedouin. But a cupful of her words are more nourishing than a kilo of chicken with prunes and almonds, *tajin jaj bi-barqooq wa-lawz;* her kisses are sweeter than cinnamon tea; her perfume is like a spell, the scent of damask rose petals; her vision is more caloric than a mound of sesame seeds. The days following my injury I was predictably downcast. Until one day, she slipped through the window of my room with a tin box from Taj al-Moulouk, a pastry shop near the hotel where the shower party will be held. There was little that I could say. It was truly a heady day. I felt as though I had gained twenty kilos in a second. But nothing could be further from the truth. I am as frail and as bitter as ever. Like carob: a ton of husk for a gram of sweetness. Ghaemi leans over me. Her fingers are velvet spiders, little ballerinas in gossamer tutus traipsing around a living statue. For the first time in days I feel the tingle of her touch on my skin. She brushes her lips over mine. Thy lips, oh my love, taste as the honeycomb: but there is more than honey and milk under thy tongue.

The shower party is a code name, the most important aspect of our stratagem. The Academy too is an epithet designed to perplex the enemy (like scallions, you have to uproot them from the stems). We adopted these names near a hideout in Kilburn, north of the Thames. It's a grenade's throw from an Irish pub where we quaffed beer every Thursday night, chatting about AK-47s, Cuba and caviar. The baby is soft, though its innocent look veils its vicious power. It proved a hot topic with Leng. "Let's use the fuse," he begged. Sadji and the cyclists were as fond of the baby: "A well-deserved present for the enemy," he said. "Now let's do a ride along the Thames." So we saddled our bicycles with pump and pannier for a scenic tour next to the river. Less than an hour into the ride I began to falter, having to lug several carob scones in my belly along with three teaspoons of salted butter. Sadji asked that I pedal slowly. At the end of the ride, I developed three blisters on my feet, each the size of a chickpea. He didn't seem to mind. Instead, he patted me on my back as if nothing had happened. "One day you'll thank me," he said. "And in a few weeks you will complete this ride in last place, with absolutely no trouble. Think of yourself as cheese, and how you will benefit from a period of *slow* change before *you're* consumed."

Sadji may not know it, but it's not only cheese that tastes better with old age. If allowed to sit, meat turns tender as lactic acid builds in the muscle. The acid destroys the walls of the lysosome, the cell body that stores a protein-attacking enzyme. Outside its home, the enzyme shows no capacity for fraternity. It goes wild and slaughters the weaker protein cells indiscriminately.

5

LOOKING GLUM, Ghaemi weighs my precious plums. She fondles them in her left palm. Each and every one of my visitors think they will provoke me from my sclerotic calm. She presses my spherical fruits, purple and bruised. She then chorals a crescendo that gently lifts my libido: "Light the fire, light the fire," she yells. My dear, let it simmer a little higher. My organ inflates like an Armagnac soufflé. Then suddenly a lump of blood coagulates in my tummy, and I fall before I can be consumed. Long before she made plans for the shower party, I wanted to marry Ghaemi. She is my private Jerusalem. But our ancient bylaws and her Uzi-armed in-laws restrict our religious union. Before my fluids reach the brim, Ghaemi pulls down my gown and covers my limbs. My unflinching eyes are unable to capture her entire figure. But I can tell that she has lunged out of the window at double speed, sprinting through the sylvan landscape, past the cedar forests and the sheep. It's just as well, because seconds later my grandfather walks in. He is dressed in wolf gray, sporting the must-have suit of Syria's secret service, the Mukhabarat. And he can be just as obvious and unyielding. Trust me, I know these things.

Family Viewing

1

MY GRANDDAD EXAMINES my face with the smug look of a re-
tired terrorist. He has lived with us since I was three, in our second-
floor apartment above Bassam's bakery. At the time, we lived in a
mixed ethnic community: a potpourri of sidewalk grocers, dusty
boutiques and paprika-pungent alleys. In the streets below us, olive-
skinned boys chased enemy bike riders with purple squirt guns. And
beyond the soot-covered minaret and synagogue, I could see the
Halavi oil refinery and the black pall it cast over the mosque.

One day my grandfather stood on our balcony wearing Roman
sandals and pajamas. He waved his hands and I looked up to the sky
to see if manna would fall. All that I could see was the sun. It was a
desert sun that had made its way into the balcony and it seemed more
daunting than any that I had seen. He then produced a pistachio-
packed sweet from his pocket. It was a rare moment when I was not

provoked by food. I stared at the sun, longing for an object bigger than candy. The heat kept working its magic upon me. Soon after, Ghaemi joined us on the balcony and Granddad grew a smile as wide as the Fertile Crescent. My eyes stayed fixed on Ghaemi. Below us, a Druze with a white beard assessed an olive tree on the opposing hill.

"I love this landscape," Ghaemi said. "You learn more about yourself and your neighbor in a place like this. You get to see what people are made of. How vicious they can be and how good and virtuous they can be. Sometimes your neighbor turns out to be your enemy, and your enemy ends up becoming your best friend."

The Druze man kept staring at the olive tree. I turned to Ghaemi. We were both a year from joining the Academy.

"Let me ask you a naive question. Why would anyone stay here?"

"Everyone stays for a reason," my grandfather said. "Some stay for the compulsion to repeat. Others because they are prisoners of their history, their homes. It's a natural thing. It may be crazy and it may be dangerous, but it's home. Should we go out for lunch now, or wait for the cease-fire?"

What makes our land such a volatile place is not that people get killed. It's that they get killed while waiting for a school bus, or they are blown apart in an open market, or they get shot eating hummus. The mundane necessities of life require that we go about our way. But we are never secure enough to be sure that that day will not be our last.

Hours later, during dinner at Cafe Ibrahim, I crunched hard into the fried fish. They exploded in different zones across my tongue. I could sense the saltiness along the front edge, the sourness along the sides, the bitterness across the back. The concentrated nerve fibers for sweetness are at the front tip. It's no easy task to steer food to the appropriate sensation strip.

I remember Grandfather would wave his hands in the air with biblical authority like Moses, but commanding more than manna. Minutes later clay plates would descend on our table: cumin-covered fava beans, grilled quail, tahini to dip the fish in and stodgy lentil stew, which my entire family loved. The memory of that dinner at Cafe Ibrahim still burns my tongue. But the food at next month's shower party will be decisively piquant, more explosive than three sticks of dynamite served in a lentil-stew pot.

2

GRANDDAD LEANS OVER MY BED and kisses my sweaty forehead. His breath is heavier than lead. I'm almost ready to sob. He looks into my eyes in order to grasp what life is like on the other side. He too is near death, and when I consider him, I see two gaping bazooka holes disguised as eyes: the same look of death in both of our eyes, the same smell of lentil stew and blood-mottled flesh grilled on the Sinai sand. When I was young, my grandfather claimed that the Spanish master Goya daubed his canvas with the fetid smell of the dying men he painted. When I told Father what Grandpa had said, he thought the story was simply splendid. It must be the reason why I prefer to keep only a three-centimeter distance between myself and a great work of art, which, like a newly cooked meal, should be the target of the nose in addition to the eye.

My grandfather waves a letter in front of my face. It's my invitation to the five-star hotel. So far from our familiar *jbail,* he's confused by the contents of the coded letter. He clears his throat and starts to read. His voice quivers and it makes me feel a little better:

To the Friends of Ghaemi:

GREETINGS.

WE COMMAND YOU, that all business and excuses being laid aside, you and each of you appear and attend before Sadji and Ghaemi and the incipient baby on Holy Sunday, the fifteenth day of October at midnight (in the morning) at said hotel to SHOWER GIFTS in this action on the part of the above-mentioned triumvirate. The party will be held in a lavish hotel where the manager spends half of his time mopping dust off the bellhops, where the waiters burnish every bottle daily and the bartender grows his own peppers for use in mixing a Bloody Mary.

Failure to comply with this subpoena is punishable as a contempt of Procreation and shall make you liable to the persons on whose behalf this subpoena was issued for a penalty not to exceed all sorrows sustained by reason of your failure to comply.

P.S. A reminder not to leave your sundry accessories behind: in particular the baby, the bike, the helmet and the hotel map.

Witness,
Honorable Ghaemi, Leng and Sadji
Attorneys for the Shower Party

3

I HAVE SPENT HOURS with Sadji observing the gray tomb that is the Bank of England. One day it may fall again, and not because of an attack on its currency, but a more fundamental assault on its bankers. Together with the gracious queen and the hunters of the mallard, they form the privileged core of English identity. Along the periphery are the impoverished classes: angry squatters, for whom cheap beef is the opium of the masses. Sadji divided these groups into hard or soft camps. His world was a constant of two consistencies. He liked his puddings hard, his targets soft.

While I trained in London, my tongue took a further turn East. It was early spring and we brewed gallons of tea: smoky Taiwan souchong, gunpowder-grade oolong, an astringent blend from Darjeeling. When Sadji felt less contempt for the Commonwealth, he drank Earl Grey. Our bias was to reject this derivative tea, so named after the prime minister of England under William the Fourth. Leading the tin boxes was Darjeeling: the Place of the Thunderbolt. To the dismay of the French, we sipped our tea with unpasteurized milk. My preference, of course, is for black *qahwa*. It inflames my nipples, unsettles my nerves. This thought is enough to rock my bed. If I could only rise from the land of the dead, I would engage the finite enemy outside my head.

4

AS THE SUN SETS, my grandfather walks out with a cedar pipe, leaving me alone in a cloud of opium. The poppies come from the Bekáa, in the East. Much of the valley has now been converted to paddy fields. A patchwork of green and amber dominates the loamy land—along with twenty thousand Syrian troops. In the mornings, they protect the garlic and cabbage fields. In the evenings, they sip rose petal tea while making sure that the ruling Baathist elite, the Alawis, have a firm grip on the agro-trade in the valley. This is where Sadji culled soft data while I trained on my bike, climbing steep hills at an escargot's speed, followed by sprints past Bekáa's pastoral fields.

Look at me now, strapped to a hospital bed, more useless than a loaf of stale bread. Visitors stare at my head, a baby swaddled in winter wool. All around me blood oozes through plastic tubes: a sanitized highway of body fluids and liquid nutrients race through me. I'm a drugged giant on an IV, an emaciated zucchini. The doctors have turned my body into a basin full of polysyllabic chemicals: an unsavory stew of painkillers to carry me into the next precarious hour. Seeing me like this, you would never guess that I'm a well-seasoned cyclist, that I've scoured continents, raced along the Loire under the luminous summer sky. You would never guess that I've spent a Sunday on the Sodom highway or followed the whistle of a Howitzer missile deep in the Shouf. My visitors look at me as if I'm a relic from another time. Except two weeks ago, my body was fighting fit. I benched 103 kilos, no sweat. I could roll boulders to the top of biblical hills while puffing a Noblesse, or better yet, a potent smack of cannabis. Look at me now. I'm unable to lift an infant let alone our mechanical baby, who we estimate will weigh more than seven kilos on the day of the shower party. It will be a big and bad baby, a destroyer of worlds.

5

TODAY I WAS ABLE to smile at my neighbor, an alcoholic in striped pajamas with a bicycle helmet mounted on his head. He is an uneasy reminder towering over my bed. His name is Hosni and he's my only source of information on who's who in the world of cycling. He leans over my bed, a wet Kent stuck to his lips. Hosni is a blend of Beirut and Bengazi, and other hotbeds of tranquility. He pulls out another Kent, working it into my lips. It's time for the BBC sports piece. Italian cyclist Romanski Prodi has taken the lead from Julien Monconduit after the Frenchman cracked his head during a hilly climb in the Massive Centrale, he tells me, hanging from his crutches wildly. Where would I be without Hosni? He then presses his fingers into my beleaguered body as if it were a mound of dough.

Seconds later a nurse walks in through the nico fumes. Hosni has had it up to his bushy eyebrows with hospital etiquette. By now he knows the protocol by rote. The nurse yells at him like a French waiter: "Never smoke for obvious reasons. Never socialize with a patient in critical care." Our byzantine hospital lacks air conditioners, so the nurse turns on a constellation of fans around us. Warm winds waft over us, blowing between her legs. I wish I had Hosni's roving eyes. Surely, they've zoomed in on the nurse's skirt, billowing toward the crescent moon, exposing her swarthy kneecaps from time to time. I like swarthy knees, more than pink ones. She wipes my face with a hot towel. I show no reaction. "How are you doing, Mr. Sphinx?" she asks.

I am the riddle she will never solve.

As the fumes clear, I see two sketchy figures. They remind me of that portrait of the farmer holding a fork, standing next to his Prozac-pining wife. I feel no connection to the bucolic landscape behind them. But I recognize that, like the incipient baby, we too go way back and form a familial triumvirate. All three of us: me, Mommy and Daddy. Instead of a fork, I'm certain my father is latched to an attaché case bulging with academic goods (he never read the cookbooks): essays on cultural competence and consumption, esoteric treaties on the esthetic disposition and how art today mirrors the free market and its denial of the social world. My dad's attaché case is his connection to the world of high art, where he spends monk-like hours peeling the writings of Bourdieu, digesting the dread and gore of Bacon. If truth be told, I would much rather chew on a strip of Canadian bacon.

I'm surprised to see my mom without her art gear. She's no doubt raised hell with the hospital about their draconian rules. The other day she told my father that it would be profoundly therapeutic if she worked on a portrait of me entitled *Deep Sleep:* a complex discourse between the painter and the patient (gouache and black crayon on canvas, mounted on wood). She is more reserved today. For once in the last three lunar months, she shows concern for my knotty needs. I crave to feel her touch against my hand. She lifts it like a squeaky crane looming over my head. I can see my left hand glide over my chest like a Boeing 747 packed with passengers. Some of them must be Swiss, sporting Longines watches and other bourgeois gear. Oh dear. Finally, my hand descends and rests next to my knee. She curls her fingers over my knee, and like an emulsifier, the weight of her hand stabilizes my body. In such circumstances, my natural tendency is to coalesce into a single and sentimental blob. I have difficulty explaining this feeling. But there is an important class of emulsifiers in cooking, among them starches and fatty acids. Chefs use them to their advantage to maintain a stable arrangement between hostile groups.

6

MY MOTHER'S BELLY is a cavernous gallery: a place where you can find stippled paint, angular planes, a furrowed brow, a domino nose, signs with hidden meanings that can be combined in different ways to build larger meanings, bigger blocs inside an ordered composition. She considers my birth a conceptual art project, an aloof experiment to see what she could get away with. Well, some experiments turn into global disasters. And I'm not talking about the polar ice caps melting. My mother hopes that one day I'll join the ranks of the World Bank. She wants me to start a family: a wife, a dog, microwave-side chats, *lukshen* lunches and two kids. But the only kid that I would ever consider adopting is the baby. My mother is in thrall to Pythagorean geometry; a peripheral circle in a remote square; a prisoner of contemporaneous and useless creativity; a closet Cubist.

Please don't misunderstand me. I have the utmost respect for my family. But I've never really felt connected to whatever it is that they were doing. During my birthday every year between the ages of seven and eleven, I received the worst presents a kid could ever get. For my seventh birthday, it was a calendar featuring the hideous art of Francis Bacon. It's the kind of gift that, on the margin, can help transform a teenager with a Gandhi-like esprit into a fierce feda'i. Spring was the part of the calendar I hated the most, especially April, May and June (one can never be too specific). April featured an office worker stuck in a corporate gulag. May was an animal lover's delight: infidel dogs with hegemonic teeth. June was the study of a chimpanzee that I thought would pounce on me every night when I went to sleep. (May God's curse be on him.)

For my eighth birthday, I remember Mother planned an amazing feast. We tasted carp, candied carrots, chickpeas and cheese. Of course, the selection will stale in comparison to our buffet: a spread of unconditional, curdled terror. We plan to serve bulbs of dismembered toes; tiny spiny vertebrae; tumescent, purple faces; tender elbows. It will be followed by blasted leg of foreign man, in stark counterpoint to the injured kumquats. There will be scattered limbs, moldering skulls next to walnuts, still intact in their protective shells. In the kitchen, where the lamb shanks are braised, the chef may come running out only to find his menu in disarray: curly endive, dandelion tossed all around. And on the hotel floor he may also find prime and lesser cuts, fingers finely ground, freshly milled pepper, a heap of cloves peeled and crushed.

The Cyclist

He who cooks poison, poison shall he eat.

I remember my eighth birthday more than any other. The dinner table overflowed with orange-flavored Miranda. An archipelago of dishes extended across the table: mounds of grape leaf rolls, cheese blintzes and pink, pickled beets. My father prefaced each toast with a five-minute sermon, evoking Mesopotamia's caliphs, tragedies and triumphs. The longer my dad's toast, the more intricate his oratory, the higher his approval rating. My father finally ended with a poetic flourish, paying homage to all the painters who hanged themselves and died of syphilis in the name of high art. It was a memorable birthday, except for the gift: a hardcover compilation of Continental cuisine.

On my ninth birthday, my parents gave me a television and we watched a documentary on the peace process. Young boys raised their arms, chanting: "Ask from us blood, we will drench you. Ask from us our soul, we will give it to you. Come give us your hand. Come let us conquer our land. Revolution until victory." Then a news bulletin flashed across the screen: a mortar bomb fired from an orchard fell into a settlement nearby, fatally wounding a baby. In response, six tanks rumbled into enemy territory. The incursion was accompanied by heavy exchanges of fire. The clashes left two girls dead. Following the program, we ate pita bread, one of the remaining symbols of national unity.

For my tenth birthday, I received a rare dictionary cross-referenced in Aramaic and Swahili. It's the sort of gift that one takes to the bathroom. Unfortunately, the only bathroom in our apartment was toilet-free, and so I had to crouch down over a hole in the ground, which made reading quite unwieldy.

Books are as common as bombings in my country, and bicycles

as scarce as Bukhari chicken stew. That is no less than a tragedy. An Arab poet once said: "To feast on chicken gives me delight. It tantalizes my taste and pleases my sight. Compared to other foods, it more than holds its own. Fit for a peasant or a king upon his throne."

7

FOR MY ELEVENTH BIRTHDAY, I finally received the best present a pubescent boy could ever want: a used touring bike with a rusty frame and a squeaky chainwheel. I stayed awake the entire night, spinning the spokes and adjusting the gears. I wiped a drop of oil from the derailleur, puffed a whiff of air into the front wheel. The bike was a Muslim green but of American make, although some of the components, like the Shimano brakes, were outsourced in Japan. I'm telling you all of this by way of background. There are more important points to keep in mind. Rule number one: you should always wear a helmet when riding a bicycle. The helmet should fit snugly. The chin strap should hold firmly against the throat. The buckle should be fastened securely.

On my eleventh birthday, I also got a stack of tattered Michelin guides from my parents' travels: photos of Bashendi, maps of Kinshasa, roads to be conquered, hills to be tamed, tropic forests that have yet to be named. *"Sur le pont de Sidon on y danse, on y danse, sur le pont de Sidon on y danse tous en rond."* It's a song I made up when I rode my bicycle across a bridge in Sidon. The bridge is 53.7 kilometers from X, and X is 62.5 kilometers from the Shouf, and the Shouf

The Cyclist

is a treacherous 71.6 kilometers from our target. The tires rolled over the asphalt; my thighs worked the pedals hard. The gears clinked: a greeting of sorts to the cedars beyond.

The Middle East may be the last place to adopt the proletarian utility of the bicycle. But it's certainly one of the first to recognize the esthetic primacy of the circle over straight lines, curves over angles, crescent moons over stripes, shapely women over slender ones. My thoughts too spin in circles. They are faulty and spent, as if they are the wheels of my broken bicycle, bruised and bent.

Preachers
in the Park

1

THE ACADEMY'S CURRICULUM was unlike any of the common colleges of the world. In addition to a survey on the Customs of Qatar, Ghaemi and I enrolled in a seminar titled "Booby Traps and Bombs." Absent from the program were classes in history. You see, if the Attorneys were busy with remembrance of things past, we would be of little threat to our enemy. History is written by the victor in the leisure of his domination. We have little time for such theoretical considerations. We remain a team of action. *Ask from us blood, we will drench you. Ask from us our soul, we will give it to you. Come, give us your hand. Together, we will wander into the entrance of our land.* So take solace from my injury. From a hospital bed, I am completely harmless. I can offer you only my fractured mind: an imperfect mosaic of memory and mishap.

My most memorable moments date back to my year of training

at the Academy. I spent much of those days saddled to a bicycle in pursuit of Sadji. "Time for a ride," he always said. "It's a clear day and you can almost see the class struggle." Our enemies were everywhere, especially at Speakers' Corner in Hyde Park. This little section of the park became an asylum for free speech in 1872. The park still attracts a wide range of preachers, shouting their unique brand of evangelism, mostly to foreign tourists who do not understand them. I went there on Sundays to monitor the opposition.

One day, I spied on a kaffiyeh-clad Croat. He stood on top of a soapbox, sharing with the world his theories on "The Surveillance Paradox": "Do you know about eavesdropping?" he ranted. "Do you know that all calls in the Middle East are monitored by the Bilderberg Group? Except for Egypt, where only incoming calls are traced."

"What's the Bilderberg Group?" asked his only audience, a teenager in combat boots.

"No one knows for sure," he said. "But Kissinger is a member. So is the pope."

I could see why Orwell, Marx and Lenin came here. It was not just to be pelted by rocks and shoes. Once they adopted a certain point of view, all of history could be made to prove it. I moved on to the next person, a visiting Taliban scholar from Afghanistan. He stood next to a polite flower. He spoke softly from the bottom of his lungs, spelling out a hierarchy of global power. The wind whistled pandemonium. The flower cringed, cowered. At the top of the scholar's list were American marines, the Russian mob and at least one Indian writer (also a criminal). In short, all of the world.

Not far off, between a gas lamp and a stately tree, a little man in a big crowd stood on a stepladder. He wore a modest robe and no jewelry. His voice was passionate and loud, but it was what he said that stirred the boisterous crowd. I took a bite into my Cadbury. I walked in the direction of the assembly. Several of the listeners wore green T-shirts that blended into the park. They were Followers of Fareed, and their eyes bore the hallmark of unwavering resolve.

"Dear brothers and sisters," Fareed exhorted, "we used to cross swords with imperialism in a sportive way, by means of culture clash, by critique and writing. But the confrontation has reached a point of no return. All veils have fallen. All barriers have broken down. Today, the enemy is right here at your doorstep, in everybody's house. Is there an Abu Bakr, an Ummah, to face him? Raise your hand if there are."

There were many Abu Bakrs and Ummahs in the crowd.

"The marines, dear brothers, are stealing the doors of your house," he went on. "And the doors of your mosque, in obstinate and open provocation. They are at our doors. Their plan is to penetrate our honor, and our values, in order to turn our society into a pervert nation, a nation of perverts. We must resist this evil current."

This is how I spent my Surveillance Sunday, every week from June until May. During the week when I was off the saddle, I escorted Sadji on foot. Lugging my weight, which was heavier than two hundred loaves of pumpernickel bread, we explored a patchwork of buildings sewn together as the London School of Economics (LSE). The Academy furnished us with a panoply of the modern soldier: we used the N/SEAS, Single Eye Acquisition Sight, a surveillance device that illuminates objects in the night. Sadji scoured the college pubs, hunting for clues among the tipsy lads. The LSE offered committed comrades, sporting Dolce & Gabbana coats. We spied at the fringes of the political spectrum. That is where we found Fareed. His followers shuttled from the LSE to Hyde Park, hawking his latest book: *The Military Studies in the War Against the Tyrants.* It covered a range of topics, from advice on how to beat a hostage to pointers on how to kill with a knife, a rope, a blunt object. (This refers to the paperback edition.)

One chapter was called "Blasting the Places of Amusement, Immorality and Sin." It even rattled the nerves under my skin. Lesson 17 offered a lethal recipe for assassination: a stew of spoiled meat, green beans and one large onion. Finally, Fareed volunteered this piece of counsel: an *agent* traveling on a secret mission should avoid argument. "Resist advocating good or denouncing evil. Keep it to yourself. Stay away from wine or fornication. And peace be on you." The book was half philosophical tract, half practical guide. It was published in a print shop on Edgware Road, where I rode my bicycle to replenish my spices: sesame seed, saffron, powdered pepper and more.

2

EVERY MONTH we spent a fortune in Harrods to launch our own jihad against the enemy. Sadji recorded our purchases under the heading of "operational expenses." As our Designer of Deception, it became routine for him to update his fashion. He binged on Daniel

The Cyclist

Hechter suits and Antonio Miro shirts. He bought a camouflage Luciano Barbera beret. The receipts tell the story best: 335 quid for a round-trip ticket to Milano, the couturista capital in the West; 471 quid for a miniskirt; 102 quid for a Cubano shirt. 1,010 quid for a Gucci collar leash. This was a gift for one of his acolytes, a nubile nymph. And what was Sadji's weak defense against this heavy corpus of evidence? Better a tawdry red head than dead. When we pressed for more, he removed his shades in indignation: "To know the enemy, you have to dress like the enemy. It's a fundamental rule of deception."

We also used code names, *potatoes* for grenades, *peppers* for pistols and *sugar* for TNT. This sort of doublespeak was necessary if only to confuse the enemy. Once we were approached by Fareed while dining at Belgo, the steamy Belgian bistro. It was spring in London and a steady drizzle covered the city outside. Inside Belgo, we chewed on mussels and mayo-smothered chips. When Ghaemi saw the enemy, she adjourned our meeting. I continued eating. Then I looked up, and Sadji had jumped on a chair, invoking Rimbaud with a theatrical flare:

"Let me go off, with my throat wearing a |Chanel| necktie of Shame, still ruminating on my boredom, sweet as *sugar* on bad teeth . . . Like the bitch after the assault of the proud doggies, licking her flank from which hangs a *pepper* . . . Oh, just men, I am sorry. But my belly is full of *potatoes*."

Perplexed and amused, Fareed walked away. In his ability to persuade, Sadji rivaled some of the best preachers at Hyde Park. Like Fareed, he spoke with conviction and zeal, and among certain constituents in our land, he commanded great appeal. Ghaemi resumed our meeting, and we returned to the topic at hand: a land mined with sectoral feud, and the most wonderful selection of fruit, the barbed-wire city of Beirut. "There are preachers in this city too," Ghaemi said. "Protect yourself." She pointed at me. "Wear a helmet. Make sure that it fits snugly. That the chin strap holds firmly against the throat. That the buckle is fastened securely."

From London
to Beirut

1

WHO KNOWS which garlic-belt European city Fareed is visiting now. Is it Greece, Spain or Italy? If he were to see me, surely he'd take me for a still life. Little would he know that I can now move my left pinkie; even entertain an erection from the sweet smell of confection. In the past two weeks, I've tussled with the urinary continence device ten times, so a system of cotton padding is used around my plums. It's no less than humiliating to see the nurse dispose of the yellow-drenched padding every morning. But I cannot help relish the disgust etched in her face. Just when she's finished pampering my penis, I squirt an extra ounce of warm piss with measured grace. My aim is to sabotage the boxes of figs sprawled on my bed. If I can't eat them, I'll scuttle each and every one of them in a pool of urine.

I am neither okra nor mallow leaf. A vegetable's chances at enlightened speech are somewhat iffy. But, as you can see, my thoughts are rather pithy. I'm something of a savant, a silent sage, if you want. I have always lacked Ghaemi's will to climb the upper rungs of the Academy. Nor did I consider crossing the line and enrolling in Moscow's Patrice Lumumba University: a training ground for elite fedd'in, including Carlos Illyich Ramírez Sánchez. You probably know him as Carlos the Jackal. But did you know that while growing up he was called El Gordo by family and friends because of his overweight physique? Yet he graduated to become a feared terrorist with considerable mystique.

That reminds me. I've added a little weight in the last two weeks. I'm now less gaunt than a supermodel on the cover of *Elle* (the Med edition); less fragile than a pink baby born in Bern. The most important thing to know about me is that my injury magnifies every sensation in my body. I feel every little thing, even the liquid Vivonex racing through me, my sole source of nutrition. The nurse adjusts the quantity to optimize my body weight and hydration every morning. Part of my existential tragedy is wrought by the region's Paleozoic medical technology. It took the doctor two weeks to recognize that the hemorrhage to my ventral pons is less severe than he originally believed. He unveiled this diagnosis after placing his dusty stethoscope against my tummy to track its rumblings.

I remember reading about a similar patient from my father's collection of books. In *The Count of Monte Cristo,* Mr. Noirtier de Villefort was depicted as a corpse with living eyes. According to the resident doctor, my injury never spread to my pre-central gyrus, the part of the brain that controls mobility. One hopes that this is a sign that I will be spared Mr. Villefort's tragedy. These grim thoughts are ruining my appetite. If I could only rest my ear against Ghaemi's belly and listen to the clockwork wrath of our seven-kilo baby. But

The Cyclist

the doctor's assistant slithers in: a vermicelli-thin nurse with oodles
of wanton noodles pretending to be hair. Will she replace the wet
padding around my penis or pilfer one of my candied baby eggplants
instead? I might as well be dead, a bullet embedded in my head.

Nurse:

"Hey, Mr. Stiffy, I see you've
been active. Why don't we change
the wet pad first and then let's
turn you on your side and I'll
slap you on the back. I want you
to cough up all the mucus that
you can to clear the lungs first.
Second, I want you to flush the
throat, and then, third, we
have a special surprise for
you: a bowl of lentil soup.
It's not for you to eat.
It's for you to smell. It's
part of our new 'home smells'
rehab program to expose your
little hairy nostrils and
sleepy senses to familiar
cooking odors. Smells from
the past, pillows to soothe
your sore limbs and all I
get is a pool of piss to
clean. Thank you very much."

You're most welcome, my pretty ogre. And I show her the pinky, a poor substitute for the middle finger. I am trying to move my metacarpal first. Since half of the bones in the body are in the hands and feet, any progress in these two areas and the rest will be easier than spitting a sunflower seed. My tendons are already busy repairing their links with my skeletal muscles. My nerve cells send hurried messages to the provinces of my limbs, anxious to revolt. If only our butcher were here, he would break my muscles out of their cloistered hold.

2

A *LAHHAM* is what the locals call a butcher without a medical degree. We had one in the village where my family spent two lunar months of the year: a tradition that began the same year Abdel Nasser ousted King Farouk. I'm still unnerved by flashbacks of the open souk. Ghastly cow heads hung from hooks dripping blood. Bundled membranes were left useless on the floor. The butcher worked the electric saw, carving shreds of my tangled memory.

Since our resort town lacked a chiropractor, the village butcher served as the resident medic. The locals queued up for hours to have him fix their backs. But my parents were blessed with nimble spines (or *spinalis thoraces* if you want to be picky), and anyway, they were more interested in the quality of his turkey. I remember my weekly bicycle trek to the butcher along a dirt road mined with pine cones, steely lizards and twigs. The trips were decreed by parental fiat and almost always included an order to buy 2.3 kilos of turkey breast, my mother's favorite kosher meal. I relished my weekly sojourn to the butcher, although I was bullied by his beard. It was a rabid red, two shades brighter than Sadji's and one centimeter higher up the cheeks. The ride took forty-three minutes to complete because of my portly physique, so when Mother was in a hurry, Father raced to the store like the slim errand boy of the Roman gods, Mercury.

I was most amazed at how the butcher stunned an animal, usually with an electrical discharge to the head. He would hang the animal from a hook and allow it to bleed. About half of the blood of a given animal is removed this way. The rest is retained in blood-rich tissues like the heart and the lungs. Possessed by a luminous fervor, our butcher killed with purpose so that his clients "would have life and have it more abundantly." Sometimes there were few buyers and the animals would be left hanging. They would suffer severe fluid loss, a process known as "weeping." Their muscles would contract, leading to rigor mortis. For the most part, the butcher was sensitive to the animals' needs. It has been known for centuries that the slightest stress on an animal before slaughter—whether from fasting, forced transport or excessive fear—results in dark meat, which is gummy in texture and tends to spoil faster. So it pays to treat animals better.

3

THE ANCIENT TOWN where I spent my summers as a young man clings to a steep hill in the Galilee. The surrounding plain brims with rooftop antennas, collective farms and olive trees. I remember ambling in the narrow streets of our village, past the pots of melissa and mint, picking some rue and rosemary. I would continue my trek, scaling the jagged stone steps next to Yasef's home. His mother was an artful cook and there was one spice which she used with reckless abandon. She was fond of the *baharat*. Arabic for spices, it consists of cinnamon, nutmeg, pepper and cloves. The scent made me wild as I climbed the steps next to their home. The path led to a tiny cave covered with creepers, a favorite retreat for mystics and white-robed *mekubalim*. They assembled at the cave every May, with their characteristic probity. Some of the visitors would light candles inside the cave, reciting passages from the Zohar, the central text of the Kabbalah. Legend has it that Rabbi Shimon Bar-Yohai and his son Eliezer hid from the Romans inside the cave for thirteen years, sustained by a nearby spring and a carob tree. Considering my penchant for a hearty meal, I am lucky to have been spared that tragedy. The surrounding fauna proved an excellent training ground for hunting *fisteyki,* tiny birds that taste best grilled, then rolled up in a warm sheet of pita and accompanied by a cool bottle of Maccabee.

My capacity for eating has always been a source of contention with the Academy chef. When I craved to nibble something new, Leng served me with the following advice: "Our shared preference for certain kinds of food has brought us together, so that we live in our own world, our own community," he said. "Now, go clean your mouth with ice. Sure, we have certain foods with conflicting claims. Falafel is one. But until the day when it's possible to resolve this dispute in a way that will satisfy the majority of people on both sides, our culinary tradition must not be compromised. If it worked for your parents, it will work for you. Chew what you know."

The Cyclist

You must think by now that I am a food fanatic. But my biggest love goes to baklava. I am open to its many layers and forms. There is the pleated sweet bread cooked over a fire of twigs in the steppes of Central Asia. The Uzbeks make the *poshkal* from ten thinly rolled sheets of dough. The Khazars bake the multilayered pastry known as the *qatlama*. My heart drums desire at the Azeri version. While the typical baklava has one hundred layers, the *baki pakhlavast* is prepared with just eight sheets of dough.

When I joined the team, we worked hard to temper my sweet temptations. With the help of Ghaemi, I shed nine kilos. I trimmed my servings of shepherd's pie in favor of beans on toast. The preparations for the shower party were more onerous than I dreamed. Ghaemi asked that I scale back my culinary field trips to Edgware Road. In the months ahead, I evolved into a health fiend, stuffing myself with bland bananas and Haifa tangerines. My favorite drink became milk packed in clear, amorphous plastic bags. I would cut the northwest end of the bag with scissors and lower it into a pitcher. Some traditions never die.

4

SADJI AND GHAEMI dropped in today with a basketful of my favorite treats. While our seemingly odd names span the troubled edges of the globe, you can trace our favorite foods to a single region. An important aspect about our cover names is that they're as real as American cuisine. During our training, we snacked on sabra: a prickly fruit outside, it's nutritious inside. As children we grew up on *choco Yotvata* and Haman's ears. The Purim pastries date back to the medieval custom of cutting off a criminal's ear before execution. This was a relatively light sentence compared to the Code of Hammurabi. He prescribes axing the offender's arms, demolishing his home, burning him, then tossing him into the nearest river.

When I joined the Attorneys, our unit's cook, the fiscally responsible Leng, hauled a fridge into our training facility. He wanted us exposed to home cooking in order to prevent any later outbreaks of dysentery. Leng supplied me with chunks of the sesame sweet halvah. The dense confection weighed almost as heavy as my Belgian bazooka.

Ghaemi runs her fingers over my stone face, pressing them into my cheeks. Sadji starts to unload the contents of the basket, laying out the dishes beside me. The first plate contains a spread of curdled yogurt, mint and paprika. Then he produces diaphanous slices of air-dried beef, as if I'm in any condition to eat. Still, I consider this gesture sadistically sweet. Sadji rests his feet on my bed. He's wearing shoresh sandals. They mean "root" in Hebrew and they have walked with him the distance into the tropics of terror. Once they marched along the periphery of Sabra, a ramshackle refugee slum outside Beirut, where he saw the massacre of Palestinians by Christian forces. Sadji is in dire need of a pedicure. His callous-plagued toes look and smell harder than an egg boiled for seven years. But he would not have it any other way. The world will always be hard or soft for him.

Not that my otherwise Rodin-chiseled feet lack their share of dead skin. There is no way around that if you want to qualify for the team. During a four-day training march from the Negev to the southern beaches of Eilat, some of us resigned. Sadji traversed the obstacle course barefoot. I was the only recruit who passed out during the marathon march, one of many tests we had to endure. But the team's psychologist viewed my commitment favorably.

Sadji has a habit of talking with his mouth full, which puts me at great risk should he cough. The last spectacle the nurse wants to see are gobs of *foūl* sliding down the network of tubes that feed my body. He scoops a piece of pita into the *foūl;* captures a fava bean mired in olive oil. The dish requires concentration to eat. But Sadji is talking faster than a road bike racing downhill.

"This is a transcript of a broadcast from *al-Jazeera,*" he nearly spits in my ear. " 'The local army today reports the capture of Colonel Bashar Boutros, collaborator and point man to a commando group which plans to attack us. The army arrested Boutros in his beachside apartment north of Byblos. Along with next-generation cell phones, a chef's apron was seized. The commando group has assumed a peculiarly Left, radical agenda. Be warned: they are not a holdover from the cold war era.' "

Sadji dips a piece of pita into the *foūl.* "They have the apron. And if they have the apron, they may be on to Leng. I suggest we change our identity." As Director of Deception, Sadji has the tough task of concealing our shared goals and aspirations. "I will miss the *Communist Manifesto,*" he tells Ghaemi. "If we're no longer a holdover from the end of the cold war, then what are we? A confessional cabal or a paramilitary insurgency? Who are we? An anticolonial gang? A quasi-state-sponsored renegade like the Maximiliano Hernández Martínez Anti-Communist Brigade? To be or not to be? And in which shape, cover or form? These are my questions. Yet I cannot give you the answer. It is not that I'm a war looking for a place to happen. But I will never miss a chance to engage the enemy. To crush him under the weight of my will."

At five foot seven, Sadji is hardly in a position to disturb one's serenity. Yet from my perspective, his ability to inflict harm seems gigantic. You have to realize that I cannot take my visitors' movements for granted. Since the doctors measure my progress in teaspoons, any setback can spoil my efforts to attend the shower party. Every time I clock twenty-four hours without a single cough, it's a victory, and I have to put everything else out of my mind in order to do simple tasks like breathe comfortably.

Full of *foūl,* Sadji wipes his hands on his jeans. He unleashes a menacing miasma, a sign of the beans. He uses smell to recognize both trail and territory. I inhale deeply, no longer able to detect the predator from the prey. Ghaemi starts to pack the plates on the tray. She suggests that Sadji spend the night in a nearby ravine, tucked between bramble and bush, then head down the mountain at dawn when the mosques echo their call to prayer. The city highway is swarming with checkpoints tonight. Sadji grabs a cookie and heads for the window, but not before pinching my cheek in sympathy. I'm not concerned about his safety: he can get bread from the inside of a rock. This is when Ghaemi dangles a carrot in front of me. It's actually a pastry in a plastic bag: "Pull through and you'll be free to eat anything you want." These words swiftly inflate my plums. My statuesque composure melts. The bed sheet ruffles. My tongue too yawns from its deep sleep, rolling up Ghaemi's crusty cheek. "I'll be back tonight," she says.

I take a deep breath. The air that rushes into my nasal cavity is warm and moist. I swallow, and my tongue retreats. The senses of taste and smell are closely linked. Both depend on the detection of dissolved molecules by sensory receptors in the nose and in the taste buds of the tongue. I think of my sartorius and temporalis, my deltoid and femoris, my pectoralis and trapezius. The names remind me of ancient city-states that were once under my voluntary control. I call on them to revolt; to shake off their shackles of captivity, to move from fixity to motion. I flex my forearm and my triceps lengthen. I bend over to one side and my vertebrae strengthen. I want to grab a loaf of sweet, leavened bread, and take the expanding power of its yeast, so that God willing, I can ride my bicycle again in the name of world peace.

5

LET'S NOT PRETEND. The shower party is the most daring mission assigned to the team. So rigorous was the training that Ghaemi insisted I ride my bicycle for three months through the steep hills of the Shouf. Careening against its cliffs, my muscles grew stiff. While riding downhill, I once lost control of the handlebar and crashed under the weight of my bike. My feet were locked in the pedal cage. There were no cars around, just kilometer after kilometer of rock, a vista of limestone and gloom. I unbuckled the straps and got up, still reeling from the force of impact. At least my head was intact. My bicycle had turned into a metal cadaver, the front wheel folded like a crepe.

Allow me here to make a small detour. As a cyclist, I'm at greater risk of injury than a sedentary passenger on a plane. Tell that to

Sadji, our paragon of prudence. He planned the details of the team's trip to Beirut with surgical precision. Ever conscious of the risks of air travel, he reserved our seats on a wide-bodied DC-10. Hijackers, he said, prefer narrow planes with fewer travelers to control. Under Sadji's codes of caution, we shunned front-row seats behind the cockpit. As ambassadors of the bourgeois elite, these passengers are at greatest risk of being hit. He then fired a broadside at me as we boarded the plane. "Remember, if someone lowers your dinner tray without your consent, it's to inhibit your mobility," he said. "And not to serve you skewered calf's liver with beans." (This is a Swiss dish, a specialty of Solothurn.)

I've learned to take such comments with a grain of salt: precaution does not prevent predestination. Sadji fears that I'll fall into an eating binge hours before delivering the cherub baby to him, whereupon we'll walk hand in hand into the hotel lobby. Yet it's he, no doubt, who may have made a pita stop tonight at a Beirut bistro, sinking his teeth into a *ma'anni*, a sour sausage tucked under a heap of wispy fries.

6

COMPARED TO BUSTLING BEIRUT, the village that I grew up in had one lonely cafe, where my family smoked wildflower-sweetened tobacco from an hourglass-shaped water pipe called a *nergilé*. The men played backgammon while discussing history. History was their bread. They lived off it. Sometimes they spoke about religion, even the Protestant Reformation. Ajmal, whose parents live in the nearby hamlet of Daliat al-Carmel, first offered the Protestant analogy. The message was revolutionary. "It's perfectly possible," Ajmal said, somewhat subdued by the *nergilé*, "for Islam to play a role similar to the Reformation, the modern force that swept corruption in the Europe." Omri, an elderly Jew and gatekeeper of the village synagogue, waved his cane. "All fundamentalists can play that role. We need vision to prepare the groundwork for something new, whether our leaders are Protestant, Muslim or Jew. But first, we have to learn to coexist." Then, turning to his neighbor, Rafiq, he plucked a proverb from his tree of many: "Better that my enemy should see good in me than I should see evil in him."

Rafiq sipped his bitter *qahwa*. "You cannot make eggs out of an omelet," he said. "This is what happens when you mix religions. Look at our village. Look at us. We were two eggs that became an omelet. We're hard to separate or divide."

Ajmal offered: "Let's make the omelet, not war."

Our family listened to these exchanges, for the most part, without taking sides. The Jews and the Druze of the Galilee share a common diplomacy. The village elders have agreed on an act of nonbelligerency. Together, we have fought our neighbors in times of war. The same cannot be said of the Golan Druze or those of Mount Lebanon. "If mountains may not come together," Mother once said, "women and men can. Otherwise, you would not have been born." With half of the clients high on cannabis—and the other half hiding behind veils of fume—few recognized us for what we were: a family of motley cultures, a ratatouille of transnational roots. *Like him who embraced Islam at noon but died in the afternoon. Neither did Moses intercede for us, nor Muhammad take any notice of us.*

Around us the hostilities brewed. Fierce patrols rumbled into the territory. There were sporadic reports of roadside bombs, bulldozed buildings, the fatal shooting of a baby. I partitioned my thoughts between this cascade of bad news and Ghaemi. We scoured the cafe from end to end, hunting for the source of its hypnotic tunes. The melodies were laced with sadness. These were Ghaemi's favorite songs, and she would play them in the morning while her mother prepared cabbage knishes. At the cafe, I remember running through tobacco clouds as the men whistled their time away, puffing at the requisite *nergilé*. Some of them were dressed in bloomers and cummerbunds, though, it must be said, it is hardly the de rigueur regalia. Others, with frayed beards, donned black felt hats and crisp white shirts; the wind tousled their curly side locks. I remember my grandfather ogled the women. They curved their hips, pursed their lips. The heat was so thick you could shoot holes through it. The patrons were prickly and loud, speaking in two languages. Sitting snugly next to these two camps—each with its distinct sense of fashion—I felt as though I was at my second home: an inverted Beirut of sorts. What glued the villagers was a love of commerce and a shifty alliance between two cultures. For years, we lived in harmony, like a loaf of *lekach* cake dunked in mint tea. Until the day our village was rocked by a bomb, and my repulsed tummy harbored revolt.

At birth, our gut is nearly revolt-free, but as we consume, we foster colonies of *Lactobacilli*. A few of these graduate to parasites and cause ferment. They rise from among a population in the millions, the vast majority of whom are innocent. However, it's quite common for tummy tensions to escalate, and for the digestive tract to want to separate the cake from the tea. In such a scenario, the two sides will find it difficult to live in harmony. The level of my intestinal stress is very much linked to Ghaemi. Of course, it's also influenced by outside events. The stress may grow or diminish depending on the ferocity of the resident microbes, and the ability of the antibodies to neutralize them.

Such Lovely
Limbs

1

THE NURSE PULLS DOWN MY JAW, then moves to the edge of the bed. My mouth hangs open, a useless hole. She lifts my ankles, pushes my knees into my chest, and gently pulls them out again. Such loving hands, such lovely limbs. My sinews expand across wadis and wastelands. And I feel dispersed in the conflicting mosaic that makes up this place. A part of my ancestry belongs to a quaint culture that does not aspire to have a nation-state, opting instead to live in peace on its fertile land. The nurse bends my left toe, now pointing to that hallowed land. And my other half, bless my mother's soul, spans centuries.

As I lay supine, the nurse-turned-yogi starts to knead my furry chest up to my neck, pressing my shoulder blades with her hands into the bed. "This will help melt the toxins trapped inside you," she says. Next, she bends my ankles again, plants my feet on the mattress.

But this time, to my surprise, she slips off her shoes and climbs on the bed. I'm gripped with fear. She bends over my face and cradles my cranium with her two hands, lifting it higher, the way my mother used to reel in her grocery-filled basket from the street merchants below. My spine lengthens. A voltaic spark jolts my body.

The nurse seems oblivious to my pain. I want to leave her with a trail of my reaffirmed existence today. By that I don't mean a streak of urine. Or a random cough. Or a fantastic fart. I want my action to be messianic, charged with eventful energy, an event that will rock the world. Or at least a hemisphere, or a capital or two. A federal building will also do. With concentration and appetite, my two hands rise from the bed. The nurse looks at me with incredulous eyes.

2

MY ARMS RISE, her mouth drops. Is that a black olive on her tongue? There is so much that I want to tell this purveyor of hope, who must have witnessed many miracles of this sort, no less epic than the parting of the Red Sea. I want to tell her to change the cotton padding around my plums twice a day instead of just once. I want to ask her if my bicycle frame is still intact, and if Ghaemi can come to see me again today. All these words stay trapped in my mouth. And then the nurse asks if I want to smell the most unwanted item on any menu: an unsavory bowl of thick lentil stew. This sort of statement can cement my sclerosis for years to come. The words are now at the tip of my tongue. My arms stay still, stretched to the ceiling.

"Have you ever been chained to a tiny chair . . . at an angle?" I strain. She shakes her head sideways. "Me neither," I say. "But that's what I feel like after two weeks." Only a hard-core masochist would pine for my kind of pain. Nearly ten seconds pass like a slow-burning fuse, and then words race through my mouth, slower, then faster, like a lonely cyclist climbing a hill. Hold still, my will.

In the days that follow, my posture improves and, with the help of the nurse, I start to crawl to the four corners of my room. Eager to engage the outside world, I begin to reconstruct my words. Like a tiny fetus I enter a period of rapid growth. I turn circles in my bed from breech position. When I can stand on my own, the nurse rewards me with a Persian pear. I bite into its tempting core. It's difficult to do, as my mandible is still sore. At night, I snuggle into my bed and think of our baby: how it will grow into a Leviathan, a giant gargoyle with grinding teeth, to chew out the inhumanity of this world.

The Baby

1

SOME BABIES SCREAM around the clock, from evening to broad daylight. This one is quiet like the desert night. That is, until we sneak it into the hotel where it will simply detonate, leaving behind a paroxysm of pain, a canvas of half bodies twisting in vain. Of course, the baby is a stealthy sobriquet chosen by the Academy to anoint the bomb. Ghaemi's son, as we've come to name our feral friend, our baby boy, weighs seven kilos. Not tall in height, but far in reach. No sense of humor. It requires little maintenance on most days, as it does not need mother's milk. Like other babies of its ilk, it can care less whether you grimace at it or leave it on its own. It needs lots of care in other ways, and if exposed to high temperatures may behave poorly. It typically attracts a daring crowd, witness my friends the Attorneys of the Shower Party, in particular the soft-spoken Leng.

Ghaemi helped spawn the baby two weeks ago after studying

the genealogy of babies at the Academy. Their origin remains obscure, though one of the earliest references dates back to Belgium in 1585. That's when the Spaniards floated four massive mines down the Scheldt River to destroy an Antwerp bridge. The mines were built on an eighty-ton pontoon and contained gunpowder encased in heavy stones. The Belgian winds blew, helping to guide the pontoon to its target. One of the mines blasted a two-hundred-foot gap in the bridge, covered with blood and bones. Ghaemi told us the story at Belgo, the Belgian bistro, where a boar steak can still be had for twelve quid.

But there is no reason why I should ruminate on Belgian boars when I have just started to chew on grape leaf rolls. What I meant to say is that our baby's target is not a bridge. It's a five-star hotel on the Beirut coast, at the bottom of a ridge.

2

OF COURSE, a preacher on the move can prove to be more elusive than a bridge. In a course titled "Mobile Encounter," we studied the errors of Johann Elser, the wandering clocksmith. He launched a bomb attack against Hitler—almost at the precise tick. During a fact-finding trip to the Munich beer hall where Hitler was due to speak, Elser felt a sensation of fullness. Soon after, he became nauseous. He noted how the bartender packed his mouth with masticated beef. What unnerved him was the way in which the bartender ate. He seemed to follow a single abiding principle: fifty chews to the mouthful, always using the same mechanical multiple. There was not a hint of desultory joy or unexpected danger in his relationship to food.

Haunted by this vision, Elser decided to build a bomb. He lived on poor man's potato and Old World yam. He carefully peeled and boiled the tuber to eliminate the poisonous alkaloid. Energized by these starchy meals, he built a powerful detonating device. On November 8, 1939, Hitler ended his speech early due to bad weather. Approximately twelve minutes after he had left, the bomb destroyed the tavern's pillar. The ceiling dropped on the spot where he had stood. Eight were killed, sixty kegs injured and hundreds of Löwenbräu mugs shattered; the tables splattered with *sauerbraten* and *spanferkel,* slices of pig roasted over flames.

"He must have built the bomb with great care," Ghaemi said. "The way you would handle a piece of sputtering butter. One wrong move and the butter burns you."

3

GHAEMI RECOUNTED THE STORY as an illustration of a mission that could go wrong. A baby is precarious, she said. It needs more than pampering. It needs cosmic intervention, or at least a combination of scientific precision and serendipitous timing. In the case of our baby, the precision was certainly there. Ghaemi had calculated the level of force needed to explode the hotel. The mathematics are complex, the values transcendental. She had even deconstructed the process of detonation during one of our meetings. One way to experience a blast is to consider a large and long cylinder of explosive material on its side. Now pretend that you are an observer inside it, she said. At first there is no sound. Your only sensation is that an explosion is about to take place. First, the pressure builds around you. Then all of a sudden the pressure jumps outward in search of oxygen. There is a great deal of heat and the atoms around you break apart. Soon, you begin to feel the tension: your skin stretches; your body swells. You can see chunks of explosive material tumbling like leaves behind a fast-moving bicycle in a highway lane. This is my path to hell. It is the road to the hotel. There will be no detour signs along the way. I promise you. Not even time to pray.

"What to some may seem like minutiae is the difference between the Attorneys and the rest," Ghaemi said, while we savored her words the way one would a thick slice of challah bread.

4

THE ATTORNEYS are a crack unit of commandos. I am the team's newest member. Generally, the best season to pluck new recruits is on their twentieth birthday, "when they are *hard*," as Sadji likes to say. My case is unusual (and so am I). I belong to a tiny Arab minority called the Druze. Although we adhere to the principles of Islam, we are not, in the strict sense of the word, Muslim. Our faith spans Sufism, Judaism, Islam and Christianity. We are known for our fierce fighters and feasts in case you don't suspect that by now. Thanks to my mother's national origin, I am the first agent assigned by the Academy to work undercover in a select group of its destabilizing teams.

Seven months before the shower party, the preparations were under way. Sadji's task is to follow the preacher, who has checked into room 201 of our chosen target. The Summerland Hotel is located along the Beirut coast. Armed with twin 12,000-gallon fuel tanks, it could easily double as a military outpost. Among its salient features are an underground bomb shelter, its own fully armed private militia and, most important from my perspective, eighteen industrial freezers, which could hold enough food to last the whole summer season. While the Summerland lacks recreational facilities for infants, I'm sure our baby's attention will be fully engaged by the fuel tanks. With a shower party this size, the staff can expect a full-frontal surprise.

Seasoned in the art of deception, Sadji has checked into the hotel as a Sudanese surgeon. Every morning he sends encrypted messages to Leng, detailing the hotel's garish guests: a mix of preachers and diplomats. "Our man is here," he would inform Leng. "We need a dozen hot *potatoes*, two mild *peppers*." Sadji would then surrender his lazy summer afternoons to the cafes along the Corniche. This is a prime stretch of land along the seafront, where Beirutis indulge their passion for cruising with little regard for cyclists.

5

THE MEASURED MESSAGE of a blast can be focused in its moral imperative. But in practical terms, its random power and reach may fail to discriminate on the basis of race, religion or creed. In spite of leaps in science, mankind lacks the technology to build super-smart bombs designed for precise ethnic cleansing, wiping out, for instance, French-speaking Belgians while preserving the country's Walloon-speaking minority. A real smart bomb would be equipped with special sensors that can tell a Swiss from a Druze on the basis of their appearance, killing one while sparing the other. A Druze head, for example, is shaved and typically covered with a white turban; while a mustache is obligatory, a beard is preferred. A bomb with morals would target only the savage. But technology is still years away from avoiding the unsavory effects of collateral damage.

The genetic makeup of the baby can be classified as postmodern kitsch. Its sensitive nature requires that it be coddled early in the morning, then swaddled in a fuzzy blanket before it's placed on the back rack of my bicycle. Its components can be traced to many time zones and places: an influence of both Occidental and Oriental tastes. Call it a transnational; there are so many of us nowadays.

It took nine days of labor to spawn the seven-kilo baby, which we have spirited with paramount secrecy into Lebanese territory, deep into its rugged hills. During the Egypt Air flight from Khartoum to Beirut, the baby was very well behaved. Strapped to Ghaemi's pregnant belly, it remained especially hush-hush under the metal detector. My only complaint: the lamb couscous they served on the flight was too tender.

It's difficult to divine whether the baby's features resemble Ghaemi. And I have observed the little critter for countless hours and from a multitude of angles. The brain is certainly Ghaemi's, no doubt. The body is a pudgy thing, not unlike the photos of my childhood growing up: a cute little darling, its burning fuse a paean of precision. Ghaemi's son, our well-preened boy, is a plastic explosive called Composition C and used by the Western military. It's white in color and resembles nougat candy. Very stable. So feel free to slap it around and it won't let out a whimper. Comp C's main advantage is not its plasticity so much as its raw power. It's 34 percent more malicious than an equal weight of TNT, sufficient to destroy Babel's tower, or a *very* tall skyscraper. Like all babies, it's stiff and difficult to work with when cold. This may be remedied by sealing it in a plastic bag, then floating it in warm water like a frozen leg of lamb. One caveat: do not attempt this last step with a toddler.

The
Attachments

1

A WELL-EQUIPPED CYCLIST should have a minimum of two water bottles and a pair of earmuffs. This is especially true if you plan to ride through the red-tiled village of Ma'asir al-Shouf. Deep inside Lebanon's mountains, Ma'asir al-Shouf is situated 1,750 meters above the Mediterranean, and in the fall the winds make it very chilly. Its peaks are home to the oldest cedar in the world—more than three thousand years old—and its strenuous slopes are sure to dehydrate the most seasoned cyclist. So it's essential when climbing the Shouf to drink water and keep warm. Of course, a cyclist has no room for a teapot or a simmering samovar in his backpack. He may instead elect to stop at the many taverns in the villages nearby where tea drinking has been a ceremonial and central activity in the rites of betrothal since the nineteenth century. During my training in the Shouf, I once crossed paths with a Syrian cyclist shuddering in the winds, brewing a pot of mint tea. He put a lump of brown sugar straight in his mouth, decanted the tea from the pot to a tin saucer and slurped it through the sugar. This process has the effect of cooling the drink more quickly while offering swift relief to the stomach. But nine out of ten dentists don't recommend it.

Compared to the Syrians, French cyclists are simply uncouth. I've witnessed a number of them toting their Hermès thermoses full of vermouth, feasting on peasant pâté during their rides, just one indication of why they've failed to win the Tour de France for a while. Unlike the French, my water bottles carry a sober concoction: a mix of lecithin and a spoon of pollinosan, a homeopathic allergy medication. It helps squelch the assault of the Levant's lovely cedars against my almond-brown eyes, a staple of the region.

Thanks to Ghaemi, lecithin is now part of my culinary rigor. It is an excellent emulsifier and prevents fat droplets from coalescing. Still, it cannot curb my craving for *kol wushkor*. The layered pastries are baked with thin sheets of phyllo dough, doused with rosewater and speckled with ground pistachio. If eating one sounds like a religious event, it's because *kol wushkor* refers to the act of "eating and giving praise to God."

But my urge for one (or eight) is steeped in a secular hedonism that has closer connections to my weight. This is admittedly an odd disclosure given my family background. I come from a culinarily mixed family, if you haven't guessed so by now. The secret beliefs of my father's people date to the eleventh century. While the tenets of the faith set strict rules on what we can eat, I habitually tiptoe into food groups that are off-limits to the rest of my family. As a general observation, my dad and his compatriots are quite fit. Their sins don't weigh on them as heavily. They're natural hikers and can be found along six mountain ranges dispersed across three countries in the Middle East. From a religious perspective, we're divided into two camps, the Juhhal, or the ignorant, and the Uqqal, the wise. The former know very little about the religion and are separated from the wise by an important attachment: the white kerchief around their headgear. My father balked at wearing one. I would have done the same. The headgear is massive. If I wore one, how would I mount a bicycle helmet on my head?

Perhaps the most important attachment for a bicycle is a quality rear seat to support much of your equipment weight, whether your load is a light picnic satchel, or as in my case, a seven-kilo baby from hell. The sturdiest racks are made of aircraft aluminum and have four-point attachments the size of M&M's. For your headlamp, you want an attention grabber. After all, when the sun sets and your road surface is smooth and your stomach is no longer rumbling, when the pine trees are asleep and the stars twinkle above the rustic hills, you may find a night ride appealing.

2

IT'S PAST MIDNIGHT on a moon-filled night and the Levant is asleep. But somewhere in this slumbering country, I'm wide awake, thinking. A cool breeze wanders through the open window of my room, then settles on the bed, next to Ghaemi. The wind is the Ebleh and it blows to the south. I take a deep breath. My chest inflates beyond its normal girth. The light from Ghaemi's flashlight droops

over my mending body. She asks about my attachments, the network
of tubes that have kept me alive all this time.

Vowels and consonants crash in my mouth like a squadron of
bats in a dark cave. Ghaemi looks at me in a daze. The fluttering sub-
sides. The disjointed letters merge to form syllables, the syllables
unite to make words, and slowly, my broken words take flight like
baby birds. With all my effort, I tell Ghaemi that the nurse has removed the tubes. I was then served a portion of chicken Chechen cut
into perfect cubes. It was a culinary crime, and the perpetrator, no
doubt, is the hospital cook who flavors the chicken with too much
thyme. Still, it was my first real meal in weeks, and I am grateful to
the nurse for working her magic upon me. Or was it the torture of
her needles stabbing my flesh that woke my tongue from its deep
sleep? I am not certain if it was, but when I saw a rotting patient
stuck to his bed, I knew I had to speak, to somehow escape the claw-
ing grip of his tragedy. According to the daily log, the first words I
spoke were "Pass me the *pepper* please."

With Ghaemi's help I have started to nibble at books again. At
first, she blew poems into my ear. Her lips dripped words like tears:
" *'Yes, all of this is sorrow, but leave a little love burning always, like
the small bulb in the room of a sleeping baby, that gives him a bit of
security.'* "

The other day, she pushed my wheelchair into the hospital library and had the good fortune to find, among the rows of books by
Malouf, Mahfouz and Gibran, a food lover's classic by *al-Warraq*.
Ghaemi carried the heavy tome back to my room and then sneaked
out the window and into the moon. That night I read the first nine
pages of the cookbook. I lost interest when *al-Warraq* insisted on the
use of new pots every time one prepared a new meal. According to

al-Warraq, if a new pot is not available, the old one should be cleaned carefully, first with mud and then with celery.

I am heartened by Ghaemi's continued interest in me. Shriveled as I am, she pushes me to expand my routine beyond reading. My central focus, however, remains eating. While I eat selectively, I have begun to compete for more than my share of food. At times, the staff has cornered me in my wheelchair, scouring the kitchen for something good. I've regained a bit of my weight, knock on wood.

"You should let me do the eating for once," Ghaemi says. I feel at ease, as if I have regained my center, my appetite.

Ghaemi slides her fingers into my plums. "Are you ready to stretch your limbs?" She takes off her civilian clothes, always one size too big. But the only attachment she's wearing tonight is a half-cup bra to lift her figs. They're fabulous and small with pointy nipples: tasty treats that tease my lips. Next, she turns her back on me, bending down. My fingers knead into her, planting almonds into the dough. What am I searching for in there? The abandoned pits from a culinary crusade? Or the life-sustaining oils for my recovery, so that one day, I'll spread terror in this foreign city without raising the broad and bushy eyebrows of the local army?

3

THE LOCAL ARMY, of course, is the highly vaunted Lebanese Defense Forces, who roam the city in their Renaults, keeping the precarious peace. Sporting fashionable green or red berets (depending on what color socks they're wearing that day), the platoons are palpable at strategic spots, namely at the port near the Corniche, where Sadji recorded the presence of eight bicycles the other day. The troops are unquestionably Lebanese, though posters of Syrian strongmen loom large next to body-piercing ads and the Hard Rock Cafe. The Academy calls this strip along the coast the Kalashnikov-Meets-Kitsch Walkway.

A bit farther down the road is the Summerland. It has a secular beach and its own live band. Many of the other beaches are named after saints, irreverent private resorts that dot the coast. There is Saint Joseph and Saint George. And then there is Saint Balash. These are names that the Christian minority bequeathed to the beaches. According to Sadji's dispatches, the Saints have turned into sewers. The coast is an undersea junkyard of car carcasses. Laziza beer bottles surf the waves, a stone's throw from the Kalashnikov kids.

The terrain is rough, even for seasoned cyclists like myself. The local forces often pull over cars for *tafteesh,* an unsavory body search or a bad session of Shiatsu, if you wish. They are paid to leave your tendons tired and tense. Then there are the bicycle merchants, hawking a spiced bread called *'asriyeh.* This is a most unusual bread. Its surface is set with sesame seeds and it has the shape of a deformed Frisbee. You can carry it like a bag, as it has a large hole in the middle. Similar to the hole in my head, an *'asriyeh* has an orifice at one end which the merchant uses to sprinkle the interior with sumac. Prodding his cart along the coast, the typical *'asriyeh* merchant is said to be an informant for the local army.

More daunting than the local army is the main highway: a heavily congested constant of humidity and honk. A web of electric wire and billboard hang over the road. When we bomb the city, candle-light dinners are de rigueur. Blackouts are more typical in the summer, often the result of retaliatory raids by a regional superpower. It's yet another hindrance that I have to cope with while riding my bicycle. A less likely threat is the occasional four-kilo trash bag hurtling down from a seventh-floor balcony. On more than one occasion has the calm of peace been ruffled by the crackling din of a plastic bag crashing into the electric lines below. Some residents along the highway still catapult their garbage, ignoring the rubbish collectors' embargo. At times the sky quakes and a jet fighter swoons, setting off a sonic boom. But more likely than not, it's the deafening sound of a Sri Lankan domestic beating a carpet on the balcony.

The skies are now safer. The main threat comes from below: the bevy of Benzes, painted pastel green and guava yellow. They rip through the city with impunity. I was struck by a Mercedes 500 SEL, next to the juice bar at Abu Faisal. A sign in front of his store reads: "Boycott the aggrieved oranges of the West. My citrus fruits have superior carpels. My melons are home to evenly dispersed seeds. My lemons shine without ethylene. My mandarins are never coated with edible wax."

It was with this same care, perhaps, that the jaunty juicer lugged my body from the street. Crumpled in his car, I jabbered a jeremiad about the lack of traffic lights in the city. But no need to take pity on me. After weeks of Ghaemi's touch, my muscles are halfway healed. During the course of a meal, I'm able to move my jaws with purpose, even disproportionate force. The localized pain in my head is now centered in my tummy, where lumps of food are anchored in a sea of gastric juice. They sit in my compartmented core waiting to be transformed to the shores of freedom. While I'm no longer in critical care,

I still struggle to maneuver without the help of a wheelchair. If provoked by the southerly winds, I'll hang from my crutches on the hospital balcony, waiting restlessly for her. I am particularly inflamed tonight, having sucked the pectin from the sticky cell walls of a plum.

4

MY FINGERS WITHDRAW from her crotch. It's a luscious strawberry turned inside out. She looks back at me, still bent; she's hardly spent. I wipe my fingers on the sheets, stained with food left by Sadji. I mount my knees on the bed. I feel as though I'm carrying a barrel of fleshy drupelets on my back. But all of this weight seems inconsequential in the face (or rather the brazen behind) of Ghaemi. And I feel as though a cumbersome load is melting from my languid body.

"My limbs are responding to your call." Before she offers a tepid "maybe" or a "well . . ." I slide my leek into her, pell-mell. "Ride me, ride me," she yells. And I think that we're both going to hell. But nothing can stop us now. My entire body is a Goliath piston; a perennial pump; a gargantuan gear moving in circles, propelling us past the giant Ferris wheel on the coast, beyond the Sunni and the surf. Will I have the nerve to deliver what they deserve? A blast bigger than Beirut, moving with ferocious speed: knocking down doors, peeling off chunks of concrete; dislodging straw umbrellas planted in the hotel's sandy cabana cove, ripping through perfectly tanned bodies, dressed and half dressed; a bellboy blown to bits; the right hand of a Yemeni yuppie doing a somersault in the hotel lobby while still holding on to a wad of (devalued) local currency: it's the lira's litany. But few events are as graphic as a bungled bomb that severs the cook's head. That's why, should the shower party end on an inconclusive note, Sadji will be on hand to spray the guests with a hail of lead.

"Ride me slowly," Ghaemi yells. Slow has always been my problem. Even my recovery has been quick (bless all the prophets). I imagine that I have mounted my bike again, cruising past the hotels along the coast, next to devout women joggers wrapped in black veil: a race between heavy tradition and svelte transcendence. Not far beyond, a preacher talks into his cell phone. It will take a grenade to pulverize his bones. A merchant sells *shaffeh,* potent black coffee served in tiny tin cups. Another vends corn on the cob. I veer my imaginary bike to the left, following Ghaemi's command. "Hold tight, just a little longer," she says. Onward to the Summerland.

5

THE SUMMERLAND HOTEL is something of an opulent retreat. There is little surrounding it, except the beach, a bank and a pharmacy. The place is otherwise an oasis. But with these nearby staples, many of its guests refuse to migrate far from its periphery. Behind the Summerland's Spartan facade, at the bottom of a steep driveway, is a pagan's paradise. Patrons enter its bunker-like doors and check in their faith in favor of arak with ice, marathon tanning sessions and a regimen of vice. Couples come here with their paramours, signing in under fake names like Sirhan Sirhan, Bibiana Beglau, Baader Meinhof and Donna Rice. This is where Sadji, may God bless his scurrilous soul, has spent no less than five weeks mingling with Beirut's best; dabbling in a bit of *kafta* and caviar; wrestling the waves on a jet ski all in the name of our explosive baby. You would think Sadji was scouring the sea for fun. He's actually looking for an undercover mermaid in neoprene or a sea urchin who may foil our plan.

The Attorneys have picked the Summerland not just for its ironic twist. What makes the hotel an impeccable hit is that it will host a religious tryst. It was different during the civil war. The Summerland was a haven for the who's who in conventional war. As automatic gunfire punctured the cadence of a sermon from a minaret, the guests refused to compromise their etiquette. With the war over, the patrons are more relaxed: high-net-worth bedouins who have embarked on a *hijra,* a journey first undertaken by Muhammad during his flight from Mecca. They come from the cool mountains where my race too begins, soaking their bronze bodies in the hotel's saltwater pools: one a resplendent replica of a waterfall, the other situated on a higher level with a strategic view of the sea. A woman, lighter than Nutella, struts around in a bikini. A little boy lolls in the sand, building castles capped with green olives, seashells and beets. Sadji has also recorded an unusual activity, mostly among the hotel's older male guests. Some of them mill around the pool fondling their crotches in a show of boorish bravado, according to the dispatches filed by our intrepid commando.

6

GHAEMI SENDS MY BODY into a pleasant shudder. Our bodies intertwine like grapevines. In the moments that follow, nothing seems to matter. Is it the tyranny of terror or the tender touch that binds us? Love may not be blind, but it's surely myopic. Consider her nose: it's a presence not worth dueling with. Still, I'm content knowing that the fluids of life in her body, when at times suffused with mine, may spawn a real baby one day, the antithesis of our mechanical miscreant: a momentous male with beady little eyes, lips more lush than the pink inside of a salmon; a tummy tender like the heart of an artichoke. And I would coddle him, then tie him to the back rack of my bike (there must be some kind of an attachment for this) and take him on a ride. I will make him wear a helmet at all times. Make sure that it fits snugly, that the chin strap holds firmly against his throat, that the buckle is fastened securely.

Ghaemi puts her socks on. I am sprawled on the sheets. With a calculating stroke she wipes two columns of sweat off my forehead, squashing salty beads of moisture dead in their track. "I'll come back again," she says. "As I always do. But when you're completely healed, walk in the direction of the cave. Our baby will be there."

My nostrils flutter. My cheeks flush. Ghaemi saunters next to my bed. She looks at me quizzically, as if I were a crossword puzzle in the *Anwar* daily. Seasoned in the world of spies (as I am in the world of spices), she has learned to improvise. "Do you remember your first bicycle?" she asks. "There was a villager who threw stones at you because you always rode in his olive groves."

In the past month, more tanks rumbled into the territory, past the olive groves, sometimes over them. Young boys took to the streets, chanting: "Ask from us blood, we will drench you. Ask from us our soul, we will give it to you. Come give us your hand. Together, we will march into our land." A fire-branding preacher had incited three self-destructing brothers into the other kingdom, sparking fierce clashes that had left seventy dead, including a Canadian cartographer who was using a nineteenth-century map of the region. Following the fighting, the preacher marshaled the masses:

"Dear brothers and sisters, our men were killed, our women were widowed, our olive groves run over. Chaste women's heads were shaved, harlots' heads were crowned, atrocities were inflicted. Our orchards burned. And so we must slaughter them like lambs. Let the Nile flow with their blood. By pen and gun, by word and bullet, by tongue and teeth."

If appetite comes with the first mouthful, a quarrel starts with a word. Considering that all things have already been said, and that all of our beliefs come from preexisting archetypes, perhaps we should all sit in silence, and enjoy a hearty bowl of tripe, without anguishing over the possibility of a common language. Let there be silence, so that we can eat our porridge, and avoid the deadly consequences of collateral damage.

"Do you remember the villager, the one who threw the stone?" Ghaemi asks. "Well, he threw them at me too every time I walked over to your house. The first time I went over, he nearly pelted me to death. I remember how you led me into the kitchen and we didn't exchange a word. We watched your father in silence, how he stacked layers of grape leaves in a deep pot. He covered the leaves with boiling water and placed a small plate on top to keep the leaves from coming apart. It was my first introduction to *waraq 'inab*. It was so good, I had to be your friend. It was the only way into your kitchen."

The next day I crossed over to the other side of the village, and Ghaemi's parents offered me an apricot. If I were to make the same journey today, would I become a target of a determined slingshot? Or should I be more alarmed that the orchards in our village are fast disappearing, and there seems to be a fruit blockade in place? Or that more than three quarters of the world's apricot output now comes from the United States? There was a time when our neighbors paid a premium for our glorious fruits, but somewhere along the way, the terms of trade moved against us, and the world became more interested in the terror that we produced.

7

IN THE SEVEN WEEKS THAT FOLLOWED, I graduated from a wheelchair to crutches, and eventually to a walking cane. At first, I was given shots of morphine to ease my pain. But on the second day of the third week, the pattern of clouds suggested a miraculous occasion. I managed to hobble into an orchard next to the hospital. With the help of my cane, I negotiated the leaves on a peach tree. The fruits smelled musty, hanging exposed below the foliage. The tree had dropped several peaches at maturity, and I managed to pick one, sinking my teeth carefully into its flesh.

At the end of the fourth week, I met Ghaemi sub rosa under the same tree. I sighed and strained as we made love under the rain. I inhaled her odor, mixed with the smell of wet soil. When we came apart, she offered a vital piece of news: the apricot boycott had thrown the region into economic paralysis, and the country had dissented into political crisis. On the second day of the fifth week, we went over the details of the shower party, and the drop-off of the baby. At the end of the same week, I walked to a cafe with my neighbor, Hosni, where we celebrated his recovery with a shot of Drambuie.

On the first day of the sixth week, I took another walk into the orchard, this time without my cane. I plucked an orange from a tree, piercing my fingers into its juice-containing vesicles, the hair-like tubes along its membranes, until the fruit bled into a deformed cluster. I pressed my fingers deeper into its carpels, the pathetic vacuoles full of sap. The hapless orange hung from my fingers like a tiny, helpless head that had lost its senses, its ability to tempt. I shook it off violently from my fingers, wiping off the torn albedo, the white coating under the peel. And then I smashed it with newfound zeal. I pressed on it further, grinding it into the ground, under the foot of my heel. On the last day of the seventh week, I knew that my terror would be real. My heart pounded with anticipation. My eyes blazed with glee. That morning I woke up, had a shower and a shave. I ate a light breakfast and avoided Hosni. I then sneaked out of the hospital, and walked in the direction of the cave.

Into the Cave

1

L ONG BEFORE W ESTERN HEGEMONY, when men were free, water flowed from the mountains into a great cave. The steady seepage of calcium-rich water (more concentrated than goat's milk) bathes the cavern to this day. At the request of the Academy, Ghaemi reviewed every aspect of the cave, chronicling its prehistoric past. This is where she asked me to come seven weeks ago to this day. In a few moments, Leng will hand me the baby. We'll remain united until death do us part.

I can hear a cello echo from the depths of the grotto. Since the war ended, concerts are held in the cavern at least once a month. Baroque is in and bullets are out. Prada suits have replaced military boots. Beirut's militias have put down the gun and picked up the gong. They have parked their tanks to play the timpani instead. But when the cellists are gone, one can hear great knells sounding trouble ahead. Perhaps it's the muffled voices of the civil war dead that echo in my head: an American marine coughing blood into his *rashidi* rice and black beans; a Palestinian in Tyre felled by sniper fire. Their shrills swell in my head, an imperial symphony of the dead. The European powers too (God's curse on them) have marched through the enigma that is Beirut. So it is only fitting that we make a similar commute.

2

FIVE OLIVE THROWS into the cave is the Attorneys' head chef, Leng. "When the sin is sweet, the repentance is not bitter," he likes to say. Was it this tasty aphorism that made me lean the Academy's way? As my senses emerged from their slumber, Leng once brought me a stealthy serving of ancillary snacks behind Ghaemi's equally succulent back. And the week after, we drank and drank, tottering on our feet, toasting my recovery with ten bottles of Maccabee, my favorite beer.

Leng is wearing thick, yellow-tinted lenses today. If truth be told, glasses are a cook's number one foe, especially in the troll-like tunnels of a grotto. In the kitchen, Leng moves with skill and skillet. Last week, he prepared a slow-cooking whiskey stew, which combines white navy beans, carrots and eggs with creamy yolks. Depending on the dish, he'll separate the egg whites from the yolks. Leng believes that egg whites form a superior foam, and that their volume expands eight times if beaten generously with a fork. Not territorial by nature, the yolks are poor at expansion. They ruin the whites, he says, which is why when frying an egg-white omelet, he must restrict their interaction. I like my eggs for their intrinsic virtue, whether they are fried, whipped or poached, separate or combined: yolk with albumen. In my eyes, all hen are created equal. Yet some have more feather than others.

3

COOKING IS LIKE CHEMISTRY. It's as much about conductivity and the ingredients that are tossed into a dish as it is about timing. From an operational point of view, our meeting is no different. All of the ingredients are in place and on time. Leng adjusts his spectacles. He slides a cinnamon-brown backpack from his shoulders, carrying it from the straps. The drop-off is running on time, smoother than a carafe of Kedem. Except there is a crucial ingredient missing. Ghaemi is nowhere to be found. Leng doesn't seem to mind. He exchanges smiles with a tilted column, walks past five stalactites: an accumulation of evil that has left a deep trace.

"I brought you something." And he sweeps bread crumbs off my shoulders.

"Is it the baby? Let me have the backpack, quick."

But Leng is tethered to the strap. He unzips a compartment and pulls out a ruffled plastic pack. It's a bag of Bamba, corn bits flavored with peanut paste.

"A little something from home. I thought you'd like it."

He hands me the backpack in haste.

"The baby is inside."

"But where is Ghaemi?"

"We don't have much time. She wants you to ride."

I thrust my hand into the backpack, feeling my way around. My fingers are frantic spiders, searching for the baby. Nestled between a jar of lentil stew and a guide to the Summerland is our plastic infant, Baby C. It's wrapped in a local daily like the sesame bread sold in the village market, where I once trundled on my bike, drawing the observing eyes of the bakers upon me.

Their mission is almost as difficult as mine.

It's hard work for a baker to make a supple dough. No matter how soft the mound, at times a baker will apply disproportionate force. In such a situation, the dough's natural reaction is to turn stiff. Once the baker removes his hands, the mound reasserts itself, and reverts to its original, comfortable form.

"You've changed shape," Leng says.

"There is more than bread in life to live for. Even with your excellent baking."

He smiles. "Good luck with everything. You'll have your bicycle soon. Just remember one rule about caution: don't be overly cautious. Now ride." He looks hardly convinced about my recovery. Like a mill on top of a windy hill, I rustle and rattle. But will I be able to produce the flour? "Stop looking so worried," I say. "All I can see now is the hotel. By tomorrow, it will burn like hell."

4

I STRAP THE BACKPACK around my shoulders and head to the exit. At the mouth of the cave, the sun distorts my view with its dense, arbitrary power. It's just me and the baby and a gaggle of Gulf sheiks, languishing under the summer sun, waiting for our vans to take us back into the smelly bowels of Beirut.

The odor of the Orient is the most potent that I have ever known. It can drive a man to die for the perfume of an orange grove. But the scent of a grilled hen can inspire one to live another day. Such is the calling of a pendulous paunch. As I consider the smell of a rotisserie, a raft of oppressive gunfire rips through the cave. Like confused cattle, a collective of humans come rushing out. A cellist slashes her bow in the air in order to clear her way. A violinist jockeys past a man in a wheelchair. A woman wrapped in a black shawl leaps into the air. She can be a ninja warrior for all I care. Another burst of brutal gunfire jolts the cave. Three armed men rush out, spraying the sky with bullets. One of them waves a chef's apron in the air to convey the seriousness of his concerns. The crowd swirls down the rugged hills. I see Sadji racing to safety, relishing the role of a terrified tourist. But there is still no sign of Leng. Nor of Ghaemi. With the baby wrapped around my back, safely tucked in the knapsack, I throw myself headlong into the crowd. Crossing a gurgling stream, the cellist in her wet platforms, we follow an overgrown trail down a steep slope until we reach the city highway.

"Who do you think they were after?" The cellist points her bow at the mountain. "We were playing a partita. Next thing I know, a man was shot."

"You were playing feverishly, I might add."

"And they shot him from the back."

"Was he wearing glasses?" I ask.

"Round-rimmed ones. A round face. A knob of a nose."

"Were the glasses tinted yellow?"

"What do you mean by that?" And she taps her bow on my healed elbow.

We walk for several minutes along the highway, then share a cab into the city. We're off to al-Hamra, the bustling commercial district. She tells the driver to drop her off at Web Cafe, where she chats on-line with her friend Fatimah. Beirut boasts the highest per capita number of Internet cafes south of Homs and north of Haifa. You find them everywhere, sprouting like shiitake mushrooms, exotic outgrowths in an unpredictable sprawl. Plowing through congested side streets, our driver engages other motorists with an unsettling discourse of curses and honks.

We drive past Starbucks.

"This city has come a long way," I say. "From blowing up Americans to running their franchises."

She collects her hair, longer than the Damascus-Beirut Highway, and flips it to the other side of her shoulder. "I just want a frappuccino."

"I think I've seen you before. What's your family name?"

"Which name do you want? Tanious Moussa, my father's? Nazli Halabi, my mother's? Ibn Salim al-Dimashqi, my husband's? How does one solve this problem?"

The Cyclist

This is the old, patriarchal Beirut. City of names, not just versions.

"My name is Nashira," she smiles. "My husband calls me Nashnoush."

A multitasker at heart, our driver switches the radio on. The speakers blare: "Ladies and gents, mesdames et messieurs, *seyidati wa sadati,* this is Radio Rasheed. Stop listening to our archenemy, Radio Fareed. Despite certain lies to the contrary, there remains a huge hunger in this country for rock and roll. I urge you to take our side. I leave you with Serge Gainsbourg's 'Bonnie and Clyde.' "

The music rips. Nashira parts her lips. We are stuck in a sea of students near Yum Yum Lunchbox and Uncle Sam's. My stomach yearns for a rack of lamb. Many of the venues here still have American names. The city seems to be saying: it's the foreign troops that we cannot digest. Yet your cultural icons, your accomplished and oily fries, your glorious and griddled pancakes, your floury and flippant waffles are more than tasty. Colonize us with your food.

"You're lucky you didn't lose your backpack," Nashira says.

"We're like a pot and a lid. Even closer than that."

"You make it sound as if your life depends on it."

The driver inspects the bag through the rearview mirror, from which hang worry beads made of lapis lazuli. I should be the one hanging there, not the beads. The cellist twists in the backseat of the cab. My only wish is to bite into her: a coriander-stuffed salmon dish. That would surely make her less skittish.

"Hope your next recital is less eventful," I say.

"I play at the Summerland on Sunday. But tonight I will pray."

From your mouth into God's ears.

"You mustn't go there. There is a shower party. All the rooms are reserved and it will be unpleasantly . . . crowded."

"I'm sure it will be fine." Nashira pays the driver in a combination of local currency and two dollars. He accepts the liras grudgingly. He prefers the currency of the Americani, even the Fransawi. They take up less space, and the pants he is wearing have tiny pockets. It's an American fashion-designer conspiracy.

"Well, it was nice meeting you. Have fun at the shower party," she says.

We are stuck in a knot of traffic. I ask the driver how he plans to move. "With a lot of honk and a bit of gas," he says.

Leng's Eulogy

(and Other Side Dishes)

1

IT'S SATURDAY and the sous-chef at the Summerland is serving a sprightly stew called *mlukhiyeh*. It's a fusion of chicken strips, *sadri* rice and mallow leaves. The sous-chef showers the rice with vinegar and lemon juice. Before serving, he layers the bowl with baked bread bits and a sediment of diced onions (shun all substitutes like scallions). Sometimes, the sous-chef alternates between three kinds of rice: *sadri, gerdeh* or *champa,* in descending order of value. The *sadri* is a slender, longer grain, while the *gerdeh* is a fatter, shorter one and certainly my favorite. The *champa* is disdained, for the most part, by connoisseurs of rice. As the name suggests, it belongs to a synthetically engineered group used in mushy soups. During religious receptions—such as this Sunday's—the hotel has been known to use imported *ambar,* a rare rice valued for its aromatic quality. Even the poultry is flown in fresh daily from the Boucherie Dureboeuf in Paris.

You may find the menu at the Summerland's shower party less savory. In honor of Leng, we'll serve well-done leg of foreign man. There will be blasted kidney *kabab* without, I am dismayed to say, corn on the cob. You may prefer Sadji's explosive treat: shrapnel-studded tongue of once gregarious kid. Or Leng's lovely side dish: pulsating heart of a five-year-old that is no longer inside her. And finally my favorite: five dozen crispy and curled bodies, courtesy of our intrepid baby. If Leng were alive, he would instruct me to save my appetite for the shower-party special: a bubbling bowl of brain bouillabaisse. This Provençal stew consists of scallops, prawns and other sea creatures, always with a touch of beurre blanc.

The driver shifts gears, racing down the coast along the Corniche. Our windows are rolled down, and I hear an explosion in the sky. It's only thunder, or perhaps it's God's cry. The wheels of the cars outside sizzle over the drizzle like grainy balls of falafel floating in a pool of oil. We pass a cyclist stooped over his bike. The driver says that he has seen at least twenty of them in the last ten days, riding up and down the coast. The other day he saw eleven riders on the mountaintops. They took a respite from the undulating peaks of the Shouf, then romped down into the maze-like roads of the city and finally to the flat, asphalt stretch along the coast, cramped with a cluster of hotels. "They are taking over the city," he says. "By the Allah's will, I will run it over each and everyone one of them." I look back and the cyclist sweeps past a ramshackle cafe on the coast. Seconds later a pack of riders glued to their bikes merge into the seaside highway. They are riding fast and furious. The driver curses at one of the men wearing a green top. I look back and the rider shrinks, tinier than a pea pod. I want to crush him with my hand. Onward to the Summerland.

2

GHAEMI'S ABSENCE from the cavern has dampened my appetite. Yet I am grateful to her for our hospital trysts. She helped stretch my muscles to their tantric limit, kneading me like a roll of dough. We were in perfect harmony, like milk mixed with honey. And how can I forget Leng's special snacks, which he envoyed past the nefarious nurse, whose only love in life must have been a ladle of legumes. Those little treats aroused my glands and massaged my senses from their sleep, even if I could not savor them at first. Without Leng, all of the caliph's camels and all of the *mukhtar*'s men could not have glued me back together again. But while my body is healed, my soul is seared. Why did Leng have to die this way? The driver darts through the highway. There are now cyclists all around us, riding in teams, wearing Beluga black jerseys. I will be among them on Sunday. As I admire them under the rain, my mind is unable to keep Leng's memory at bay. So I compose a eulogy in the backseat of the taxi to consecrate this tragic Saturday.

To the Friends of Ghaemi:

GREETINGS:

> *Our dearest friend, Leng: Though you may now be buried deep inside the darkest of cavities, pressed between the Pantheon of the Gods and other calciferous rods, the baby is safely in my custody. For each of the twenty-seven innocent lives they*

claimed, we'll maim eighty-one of theirs. Due to efficiencies in technology, consider the new math of our generation: not an eye for an eye, but three for one; a broken limb for a bruised one, multiplied by three and divided by one.

Our dearest friend, Leng. I wish you were with us to attend the shower party. Could there be a more appropriate response to the village tragedy? Do you remember the blast, the roster of revulsion? Twenty-seven corpses of various firmness and form: twelve dismembered limbs, four charred feet (two under the tender age of seven), five mutilated hands (three with rings wrapped around them) splattered across the village souk. The headlines blared: a country's tragedy. And so we must now take a stand. Onward to the Summerland.

The millstones rumble when the wheat is ground.

3

WE'RE LISTENING TO A BALLAD by one of Beirut's basement bands. It's a sweet-and-sour lullaby for our baby, who in twenty-four hours will give the last wake-up call to drowsy guests traipsing in the lobby. Pleased as a peach, the driver sinks his teeth into a perfumed plum, having left the riders behind. What does that plum portend, so sweet and soft? It's more supple than a nurse's caress, a deeper purple than the healed bruises on my face. He bites into its ripeness, and the plum plunges to its death, into the decay and decadence that awaits us all.

The Cyclist

"You have an accent," he says.

"My father is Druze. But I studied in Europe for a while."

"I went to the university of General Aoun," he laughs. "We worked with the bombs instead of the books because we are part of the people of here. This is why we fight. But peace is much better. I have the family now. And if not for all the bicycles in the past ten days, I have to say the driving is safer."

"There is a race tomorrow, from the mountains to the city."

"The mountains to the city?"

"It's not so strange," I say.

"How so?"

"I mean, you do everything in reverse here."

"This is the truth." And he spits the plum seed on the dashboard. "The downhill is better than the uphill. But the roads are slippery, as you can see it, and the city is built like the maze. So we like to take the shortcut when we can."

He veers to the left unexpectedly and the worry beads swing wildly.

"Where to?"

Perhaps we should drive back to the cave. We could lift Leng's body from inside the cavern, against all odds. We could then speed south to Tyre and Cana, where Jesus turned water into wine. With Leng locked in the trunk of the car and the wind blowing at my plaintive profile, we could continue our trek, inching ever closer to safety, into the arms of the Galilee. But the risk of salvaging Leng's body would hardly justify the journey. You see, the border between our countries is shut. The hermetic hamlets in the south are a cradle of hostility. And with everything said, Leng is dead. I must press on to the Summerland.

4

THE DRIVER DROPS ME OFF along the demarcation that once split the city between Christian East and Muslim West. This is where I had my bicycle accident. During the civil war, the militias drew a green line through the district all the way to the seashore. Sadji has reviewed countless recon photos from our jets documenting the protean profile of this place. By the end of the war, the green line had grown into its name. Snipers moved into blighted buildings on opposing sides of the line. They peered at each other through leafy trees and looping vines. One of my favorite photos is of a sniper nestled in his nest, trimming moss and preening plants.

When the war ended, a Muslim merchant set up a makeshift cafe with plastic chairs in the middle of the rubble. His patrons came from all over Beirut. They sipped coffee from tiny cups under Cinzano parasols. Sadji would pick out the foreign spies from the bedouins and bankers. Unlike the local mob, they always ordered the crème espresso double. There are no more ruins to be found here. Seven olive throws from where I stand is the famed juicer who hoisted me to the hospital in my time of need, may God bless his soul. I am here to tell him to avoid the Summerland on Sunday. It's the least I can do, considering he saved my life. All around me, the buildings, once completely mauled, have undergone an overhaul. The district has transformed itself once more. But etched into the new limestone walls are bullet scars that the architects have left intact as permanent reminders of the past.

The Cyclist

I make my way to the juice bar, the baby tucked in the knapsack. Inside, Abu Faisal, the portly proprietor, considers the pulp of a papaya, ready for the blender. When the war still raged, the district's denizens went to the bar for friendly chats around the blender. The juices regulated their nerves and brought them closer together. But for all its profound fusion (not to mention its mayhem and confusion), the place is not without its antics. For one, all the shakes are named after depraved despots. In the current season, the emphasis is on Latin American rogues. First on the list is Manuel Noriega: a tropical blend of pineapple, papaya and milk. Next is Alfredo Astiz: a plum puree mixed with goat's milk and anise. Astiz is an Argentine officer charged for the death and torture of two French nuns. The proprietor will tell you that the drink is served with two cherries on top for sweet symbolism and fun. Like everything in the Middle East, even a papaya is informed by politics.

On the wall behind the counter hangs a black-and-white photo of the juicer's grandfather. As I try to peel his past, the jaunty juicer waves at me from behind the blender. He smiles, and his lips curl in the shape of a banana, bland and benign. Less than four months ago, he must have confused me with a Druze having a bruise, a heap of broken bones that he scooped from the street into his guava-yellow Mercedes 230. If he had known who I was, he surely would not have taken me to the hospital. I have difficulty recalling the moment of impact. I remember the car sped my way, its headlights trained on my shivering bike. After the crash, I was in the backseat of the juicer's car next to a crateful of limes, heading to the hospital.

"My boy, look at you. Your cheeks are like the rosebuds."

"And what were they like before?"

"A broken hazelnut," he laughs.

"I want to thank you for helping me."

Sometimes a kind word is better than alms.

"My boy, what were you doing on the bicycle?"

"Training for tomorrow's race."

"I've seen so many bicycles in the last two weeks. Each time I saw one I'm thinking of you."

"Will tomorrow be a busy day for you?"

"Allah is willing. But not because of your crazy race. I'm working the Summerland tomorrow and we have to lock up the store."

He switches the blender into high gear. I can barely hear him through the din.

"Did you say the Summerland?"

"Is the only place I close my shop for."

He points his left index finger to his right ear in a sign that he cannot hear.

"Please, put it down, your bag, and have the drink," he screams.

"You saved my life."

"You are the most welcome. Thanks be to Allah."

He throws a fleet of figs and a bounty of Brazils into the blender.

"Why is it you never told me your name? The picture behind me is my grandfather, al-Wazzan. We call him the Weigher of Plums."

In the Middle East, Arabs select their names carefully. And the names often have a meaning. Muhammad means the praised one; Maher, the clever one; Saleem, the cautious one; Bassam, the smiling one; Adel, the just one; Shaheed, the one destined to martyrdom. Our names have meanings too. But I never told the juicer my name. Not even my nom de guerre, a cover name like Leng or Sadji. It's easy to betray one's enemy. But how could I lie to the man who picked up my broken sprawl in the alley? I saw death with my own eyes, and it was not through corrective lenses. With the baby glued to my back I leave the plethora of plums behind, waving the juicer good-bye. "May Allah be with you and that you ride with the speed of an arrow," he cries. Outside the store I feel heavy, saddled with the weight of sorrow. I shall have to kill this man at the Summerland tomorrow. Without his help that would not have been possible. And I am palpably provoked by his act (even grateful, if I may say so), for when an event happens on which you did not count, it behooves you to snatch the occasion that a kindly fate offers. I shall spare you the lies, Abu Faisal: we are neither Attorneys nor is there a shower party. I would have preferred that we became friends. But as Mobutu Sese Seko cautioned: "Without smashing some *coconuts,* the world would be a more violent place."

Sweet
Temptations

1

IF YOU'RE AN INSECT, death is the delicious dessert that always comes last. But those poor little pests must have had a foretaste of my rotten remains. Feeling rejected, I came back together with my split helmet. Of course, I'm not the only cyclist who has dodged death. During the 1974 Tour de France, a carrot-haired Dutchman named Joop Zoetemelk survived a similar fate. He hurtled into a parked car and cracked open his head. It's a wonder that he ever walked again. Yet nine months later he won Paris-Nice: the race to the sun.

Tomorrow's race starts from Lebanon's alps and descends to the coast. I've been asked to ride leisurely, slower than the boy who went to fetch mulberry leaves for the silkworms: when he came back he found out that they had already made cocoons. My instructions are to move at maple-syrup speed. After one hour I will fall behind all of the other riders. I'll then break away from the pack, alone with the cedar trees that dot the mountains. This is a difficult concession for me to make. Since the age of eleven—when my parents gave me my first bicycle—I have always wanted to win a race. That dream will have to wait until another day. Once I'm clear of the army checkpoints along the coast, I shall have to ride to the hotel instead. I will then deliver the puckered baby to Sadji, who will be waiting for me in the hotel lobby. Soon after, the wires will report the lurid details of the tragedy: "Bomb Blast Rocks the Summerland, 357 Dead Including the Head Chef." It's a delicate plan and there are many hazards along the way.

2

FOUR OLIVE THROWS from the juice bar, I spot a red-haired man mounted on a Bianchi, pedaling away from me. He disappears into the rain, a slippery sop wallowing in a thick stew. Is it my mind playing tricks on me? I walk past a mosque near Rue Allenby, and there is no sign of him. But I feel as though he has always escorted me, watching me, goading me on, pursuing each and every one of my steps without making himself known to me. Like a pot and a lid: we are closer than that. I hide the baby under my coat to shield him from the drizzle. We don't want the grotty streets of Beirut to enervate his constitution. All good parents tend after their offspring, and our young prince is no exception. After all, the last grape on the cluster is the sweetest, and the youngest child in the family is the dearest.

The Cyclist

The hours fly by like doves in the sky. The drizzle has stopped. It is dusk, almost dinnertime. I walk past a street vendor, clinking tin cups on his fingers. He chants in delicious languor: " '*Irq al-soos, 'irq al-soos*, the best licorice drink you will find south of Damascus." But my stomach yearns for a noodle kugel. Please excuse my gluttonous rambling. It's just my stomach rumbling. If truth be told, I have lost thirty kilos during my sojourn in the hospital. For a sybaritic soul like myself, convalescence has meant tortured bouts of withdrawal. I have had to abstain from sweet temptations: notably, the *tamir mahshi,* dates stuffed with almonds. Not to mention the crispy (some would say tooth-shattering) *ingberlach:* a honey-nut candy spiced with ginger and sesame. How I miss being part of the cookie cognoscenti! In the Talmud, it is said that honey and sweet foods enlighten the eyes of a man. With me one cannot tell. Perhaps it's because I like to wear shades. Or because my injury has dimmed the shimmer in my eyes. Or simply because the world looks more bleak than an over-boiled leek when one has to kill.

3

IN HER LATEST COMMUNIQUÉ, Ghaemi praised the precision of my palate. I had finally graduated from being a gourmand to a gourmet, she said. A gourmand is an excessive eater, while a gourmet is a connoisseur of food. Call me what you will, it is almost dinnertime. I kick a Koura, an empty can of olive oil. I head to the coast. There are strollers and bicycles parked along the sidewalk overlooking the sea, young couples lugging their babies, just like me. The waves crash and the salty spray stings my tongue. In an hour, the fishermen will light the lanterns in their tiny boats and head to the shore with the fresh catch of the day: fleshy mullet called Sultan Ibrahim. My thoughts turn dim. I stake a spot next to a row of BMWs. The smell of costly cologne fills the air. Welcome to Beirut's Bacchus belt. Here you'll find wealthy Kuwaitis that the orphans of war wish they could pelt.

As I unstrap my backpack, three cyclists drift along the coast. Seconds later, the man with the red hair glides by again. This is no random event falling from the sky. It is an apparition, an inexplicable act like manna falling from above. Father always said: a lark never drops into one's mouth ready and roasted unless there is a reason for it. I look above and the rain has long since stopped. But the cyclists are still wet, more sodden than scraps of pumpernickel in a teeming stew. Fortunately, Leng had the foresight to shield the baby from the rain. After concealing the infant in a newspaper, he stuffed it in a plastic pouch. Next to our errant child is a jar of lentil stew. The ancient Egyptians believed that lentils would enlighten the mind and open the heart. The Catholics swooned at the scent of Lent. The Romans claimed that lentils made men reserved and indolent.

My distaste for the pesky peas is confined to the red ones, which are actually orange when hulled. For my mother, those pathetic peas held a larger totemic appeal. She would bathe them carefully before preparing that baneful brew. I stayed away from the kitchen on those steamy days. According to tradition, Jacob made the red potage in memory of his grandfather Abraham, who had just died. I once asked Mother about the lentils. She said: "Just as the lentil is round, so mourning comes round to all the denizens of the world." Or perhaps it's because worries are easier to bear with soup than without it. That is why lentil dishes are traditionally served as the meal of consolation following a funeral and at the meal before the fast. Death is hunger and hunger is death and a pot of peas has plenty to do with both of them. So it is with caution that I open the jar and gulp down its contents. To my surprise, it's hardly stodgy. Perhaps I need to purge my palate of its trite taboos; unacquire my tastes; try new ones. What better way to understand that there is more to life than blowing up the Summerland. Instead, I could sample morel mushroom toasts one day; or grilled endive with sauce Gribiche; a crusty thyme bread called *manaish;* a (sparing) portion of jellied eel: the perfect colonial meal; I will even consider a hegemonic burger from the Occident.

4

HAVING DESERTED THE PACK OF RIDERS, he peers at me through his pungent breath. He takes out a notebook and scribbles in it, the doyen of death. Barricaded behind his bicycle, he looks at me again. I am hardly moved at being the target of his screening eyes. Observation is common practice in my line of work. It is more than 93 percent of what we do. The remaining 7 percent is what I have trained for in the Shouf. In the hospital, I was observed by more than one hundred eyes, curious to see if I would wink. Little did they know that I could still think. Or see them more clearly than the desert moon. I remember one day Ghaemi pressed her fingers into my beleaguered body as if it were a mound of dough. I stared back at her like the Sphinx.

I continue eating as if nothing has come to pass. He continues his cold examination, increasingly crass. Some men are so prying: they would smell your apron strings to guess what you've cooked for dinner. Well, come a little closer, my friend. Inhale. I am the aromatic scent of death; a soupçon of sin; the sweet smell of a severed limb. I catch a glimpse of his ruddy cheeks. They are vital, like the pomegranates in our literature and lore: their shape woven into the robes of the high priest, etched into the temple's pillar and ancient coins. He puts the notebook away. He takes off his helmet, exposing his crimson hair. He strolls toward me, escorting the road bike at his side like a beautiful bride. I pretend not to see him. But he wants to be seen. He rests his bicycle next to my feet. They say that an image is worth a thousand words. But what if the words are encrypted in digital code? It would take a thousand technicians to decipher the identity of this man.

The man with the red hair reaches out and grips my shoulder. I take a step back, completely absorbed by his bicycle. It is the identical twin of the one on which I trained. Except this one is new and without a dent: no trace of an accident. Just a few streaks of mud and rain here and there. It sleeps on its side. The front wheel spins in circles, slower and slower. Not quite like my thoughts, which unravel like an *S,* only to turn linear. They sprint past the roadblocks of time: first, the beaming headlights of the car; then the force of impact, followed by a hellish honk, still howling in my ears. All of these moments are mired in my mind, swinging like a pendulum from the present to the past. Sometimes a piece of ill luck comes in handy. This is the lesson that I have learned from my injury: from now on, when

The Cyclist

I ride a bicycle, I will always err on the side of caution. I will make sure that the helmet fits snugly. That the chin strap holds firmly against the throat. That the buckle is fastened securely. As I emerge from my startled senses, the man with the red hair throws his sweaty arms around me.

"Never mind the disguise," he smiles. "It's me, Sadji. Terribly hurt that you didn't recognize me."

Beirut's B 018

1

I WANT TO PICK UP Sadji's helmet as if it's an archeological find: an august relic or symbol of truth.

"I've brought you a present from the Academy," he says. With Sadji the hint always hits harder than the truth. Why would he offer me a present so far from home, unless it was the preface to something that was much more troublesome.

"The bicycle is for you. We want you to use it in tomorrow's race."

I look down the highway and I see a silver rush of spokes. Sadji lifts the bicycle and offers it to me.

"Do you remember your instructions to ride after me? That was my idea, actually. It was the most effective bait to curb your weight. We've done a fine job of chiseling you into shape."

"Except the weight of this mission is enough to crush me."

"You'll do quite well, I am sure of it."

"Then what a poor choice you've made. You could have picked a more able agent to ride to the hotel. Why make me go through all of this hell?"

"Because you're half Druze, remember? And you have a bruise that hardly makes you suspicious. And because your goal is not to win the race but to deliver the baby to the hotel."

If a face tells the secret, one would never know it by his look. Not a timorous twitch or a pinch of passion. He has the zest of a zucchini. And he is as lean as one too.

"You know, we never pick the best candidate. Only the one best *fitting* for the job."

"You're a great storyteller," I tell him. "But no need to go on. I'll find a fortune-teller to guess what you are going to say next."

"Don't forget the bicycle!" he yells. "Do you remember all those rides we took around Hampstead Heath while you gritted your teeth? I would ask you to moderate your speed. Remember one thing: tomorrow you shall never take the lead."

"We've gone over this. I'm walking away."

"And one more thing," he says, and hands me his helmet. "You can walk away from me now if you choose. But you can't outrun the moon."

I look above and there is the moon in all its brightness. When the moon appeared as a curved silver, my father always came to see me. "Let me look at the moon on your face," he'd say. He would then make a wish. I look into Sadji's face. For the first time, I see that it is fraught with the force of a thousand soldiers. What if I wished that we beat our barbed wires into the Good Fence; recycle our bombshells into potted plants; succumb our spears to the will of pruning hooks? Perhaps then we would devote more time to organizing exchange programs for our region's cooks, and peace would be more than a passing reference one reads in books.

Sadji says: "If you still have doubts, come to B 018 at twenty to ten. We'll drink nectar from Kefraya. Toast Leng. And as a special treat, I will make sure that Ghaemi is there."

He then walks away in the direction of the Summerland. Off to run a pre-shower-party errand? Consider the efficacy of a fuse? Locate a timer or fine-tune a percussion primer? Will he lead a forensic foray into the back room of the hotel to make sure that the baby gets there safe and well? Ghaemi would certainly know. I strap on the helmet and mount the saddle. I make sure the baby is lashed onto me safely. I start to pedal along the coast, away from Sadji. The tires roll over the asphalt; my thighs work the pedals hard; the gears clink: a mechanical greeting to the cedars beyond.

2

BEFORE I RIDE TO B 018, there is one thing that I must do. I know, I know, I just had a serving of Leng's lentil stew. But you must forgive me. Tomorrow is the big day, and my appetite is almost as big. I decide to head to Ras Beirut, the head of the city, which is a knob of land that stretches into the sea. The breeze there is always salty. I walk into an Internet cafe on Rue Samadi, where Arabs puff their water pipes in peace. They smoke slowly, then send a flurry of electronic messages at the speed of light. In the whirl that is Beirut, tradition is a close ally of technology.

To my dismay, the snacks at Net Cafe are less than savory. The menu is a *mezze* of mealy fries and fried liver. There is *baba ghannooj,* or "spoiled old daddy," so named because its inventor is said to have mashed the eggplant to its pulp to pamper her old and toothless father. When properly garnished, it is as pleasing to the eye as it is to the palate. But at Net Cafe, you are better off with a salad.

Saleem, the cautious proprietor, assigns me to a station. "If you are intending to transmit a vast volume of digital data, you are comin' at the wrong place," he says. "Yesterday, somebody blew up the undersea cable."

Another day in the Middle East I think, another conspiracy fable. Another ten thousand full moons have to come and go before the region is stable.

Saleem asks to search my backpack. It's a routine check the store adopted after a car bomb shattered two of their computers on Monday. "It was rocking the entire floor," he says. "Bits of the computer went off into the ether. It was a rival Arab gang who started this things. So much dirt buried under our carpet. But it is okay, you know, because blood between Arab brothers, you can never turn it into water." He shrugs. "My brother will always be my brother, no matter how much the difference I have with him."

Saleem rifles through my bag, cautiously. He pulls out the baby from inside a plastic pouch like a pudgy newborn entering the world. He unwraps the newspaper, kneading his fingers into the bomb. "What is this?" he asks. "Your lunch?"

"I would never eat such a thing," I say. "My mother is a sculptor. She works with clay."

He offers a sympathetic smile. A lie will travel a mile. "Take a seat then. You must accept my sorries for your trouble."

I look around. Everyone is tethered to a little bright screen. Saleem stares into his laptop in a trance. One of the patrons puffs on a water pipe: a well-deserved respite. He looks at me, then continues to type. It's time that I check the latest news from my family.

3

FOR YOUR CONVENIENCE, I am passing on to you, word for word, what has been sent to me via electronic mail. More damning doggerel from my mother. You must excuse her, for she is a painter, after all.

To My Dearest Son, My Geopolitical Child:

We met your friend recently. He's a freckle-faced redhead named Sadji. He said he knew you from the Academy, then promptly delivered the news about your accident. Never have I met anyone so larger than life, like a daring David (the marble one and not the bronze). He helped arrange our papers and whisked us to a certain city (I am uncertain which) and then across the border into your company.

This being said, you should be especially proud of your father. If it were not for him, that delightful and dogged Druze, we would not have set foot in the hospital. How easily he blends into a foreign land, and into the mountains and the ivory-hued stones, the cedars and the rusty red-tiled roofs as if they are his own. I am doing a portrait of it all. But what you must know is that we visited you every day, undeterred by the suspicious looks of the nurse, and under the direction of the Academy. They really wanted you to get well, almost as much as me. But what I want to tell you is that the hospital did not suspect a thing. Your nurse invited us over for mint tea. The Academy advised us not to go. Well, our hearts may be small, but together they embrace the world, and there is just one more thing I want to say, which is my wish for your quick recovery. We would have stayed longer, you must take my word, but there was a complication with your friend Leng, and so the Academy wanted us to leave in secret, without a trace. Sadji was kind enough to inform us of your recovery.

My Dearest Son, My Transnational Child, a plaintive poet once said: "There is hidden sweetness in the stomach's emptiness." When I saw you in the hospital stuck to a ramshackle bed, you looked gaunt and underfed, and I sensed the sweetness inside your empty tummy, and it was more yummy than a broth of cabbages. You are sweeter than sugar dissolved in milk.

All the best, wherever you may be.
Your Mother, The Lesser Patriot

The Cyclist

Such tender words (more saccharine than sin) have the effect of sending sparks through my skin. A dizzy hunger sets hold inside me. Outside the cafe, a pall of prayer comforts the city from the high towers of the holy mosques. The streets bustle with kinetic energy: a mayhem that resembles the unbridled blast of a bomb. As I mount my bicycle, my nostrils seize the scent of a honey bun. Just like the knotty *zemmel* or the sweet *bulke,* the braided rolls, that Mother baked for her wayward son.

Before I head to B 018, there is really one last thing that I must do: dinner for two. That is, two plates of everything on the menu. For this may be my last supper before the baby delivers its billowing blast, erasing my future and my past. As for the present, there is nothing like it. Everything erased in a screeching second: my dismembered body intertwined with hundreds of other vital organs, like grapevines; my blood suffused with theirs. Just like strangers who cling in a moment of tragedy, exchanging sympathy. Can you think of a more intimate union with the enemy? So what if it's in imperfect pieces after we are mangled and maimed. A geography of harmony. Seconds after the blast, my corpse may end up at the center of a new world map. It may already be too late to tamper with my fate. So once I am dead my wish is that my remains are sprinkled into the Med. Surely, a pinch of my powdered pinky is enough to make all of the fish in the sea happy. My dear little fish, whether you are a gelatinous gefilte or a ponderous pike, I have one thing to tell you: eat me at lunch before I eat you at supper.

4

SOMETIMES DEATH DESCENDS UPON US. At other times, you just have to nip it from the rosebush. But what if along the way I am stung by a prickly stem? Or led by the smell of a brioche into the heady heat of a bakery? What if I shift my will while racing down-hill? Or lean left on my bicycle's handlebar so that I find myself in front of a fast-food stand, completely removed from the Summer-land? Please don't misunderstand me. It is not that I am afraid of that other kingdom. But I am certain that my enemy too has weighed the value of martyrdom. Or questioned whether this road to death is better than the accidental one. Even if it was for a fleeting moment. Do not mistake this for a case of cowardice or that ephemeral fear that visits the most committed of us. Behind our hardened shell, thicker than a walnut's, we are human just like you. And while our senses have been conditioned to withstand a bomb's explosive wrath, my preference is to be showered with calamus and cinnamon, myrrh and aloes, with all the chief spices in a fantastic bubble bath. Is my counterpart, the enemy on the other side, also plagued with such frail thoughts?

It takes years of mental training to believe that one could kill oneself as a way of killing the enemy. Here is what would happen if I took my life along with the baby: the number of victims would in-crease exponentially. The mathematics are complex, the target tran-scendental. I can see the headline already: "Suicide Bomber Rides into Hotel, Kills 350." The number of course is arbitrary. And I have veered off from our original plan. Ghaemi will not be happy should I cross that undeviating line. But I have already danced with death from a hospital bed. I have seen its intimating shadow with my unflinching eyes. When I lost control of my body, I lost the little power I had in the world. How much I wanted to burst in a flurry, flailing my arms and legs. Or to feed myself with a regular fork and spoon and set my will free. To die in a hospital bed is the worst kind of death. Your thoughts become synchronized with your breath. As you wrestle with your health, you begin to ruminate, framing portraits from the past. The only time I was able to protrude my tongue, I let out a purulent spit.

Now I can do much more than huff at the enemy. I can take extraordinary action and abandon our baby in a remote shed. Let us ride to the red-orange fields instead. There I would sift saffron from the purple crocus. Since it requires more than eighty thousand blossoms to produce half a kilo of saffron, it remains the world's most expensive spice. I would give up my most prized of possessions—even my soul—for a bowl of saffron rice; its yellow stigma stinging my eyes as if I were in a trance; its bitter threads, more brilliant than a soft quince, coming to my defense.

5

PERCHED ON MY BICYCLE, I roll down Rue Samadi lugging the singular weight of my hunger. It is almost heavier than the baby on my back. We pedal our way past a kaleidoscope of cultures: on the sidewalk a frayed philistine hawks soap made with olive oil; a street merchant sells handcrafted crosses from a gold chain; a woman veiled in dark green offers buckets of bulgur and other grains. When I am hungry, my senses are rushed with wild and spasmodic pain. The only cure is the enchanting taste of saffron and the scent of crushed nutmeg. I roll down the street, my stomach rumbling.

I must have my last supper at Marroush. It's a cavernous space: a pleasant place for a feast. Inside, a caged parrot mimics the incoming whistle of a howitzer missile: a trick she learned from the civil war days when the city had to endure more than the occasional drizzle. A portly waiter serves sliced pita in a plastic bag, a plate of turnips under a heap of crushed ice, the perfect pickles. The hallmark plate on the menu is a Turkish dish called *imam bayaldi*. It means "the cleric has fainted." It is a marriage between baked tomato and eggplant that, according to legend, caused the holy imam to faint when he ate it. The eggplant is certainly good enough to make one pant. I can hear the imam above Marroush. He is very much awake, chanting holy prayers, quoting passages from his latest book, *The Military Studies in the War Against the Tyrants* (now in hardcover). He instructs his followers to oppose the renegade regimes and their crusader centers, the Masonic lodges and the Rotary Clubs. Potential targets include the Cambridge Cricket Club Granta and the Partisans of Polenta, whether Italian or not.

"Dear brothers," his voice thunders. "We used to cross swords with imperialism in a sportive way, by means of culture, by critique and writing. We must now graduate to another form of fighting. The confrontation that I'm calling for today does not know Socratic debates, Platonic ideals nor Aristotelian diplomacy. It only knows the undoing of the apostate enemy. By pen and gun, by word and bullet, by tongue and teeth. Can you see the infidels nailed in the wooden box underneath? Silenced in their coffin, yet still dreaming destruction, weaving a diplomacy of disarray. They dare not take the move against us."

6

IF ONE IS PAYING for the meal, one may eat and stare at every dish. So I ask the waiter to bring a pair of every plate before I ride to B 018. I am ready to eat the egg and its shell. Soon after, he spreads the table with a foretaste of the delights to come: two sumac-flavored spinach pies named *fatayir;* two chickpea patties known as *kibbet* hummus served with two bottles of Laziza beer; a pair of fried eggplants anoint the *batinjan maqlee.* Just like the animals on Noah's Ark before the great storm, everything in pairs: two vessels of fava beans with Egyptian tomatoes, called *tomatim:* as you can tell from my appetite, I am trying hard to remain trim; two helpings of *maaloobeh:* a dish prepared with eggplant, cauliflower, rice and lamb, which I prefer to Westphalian ham.

While in most Western cultures dinner is an immutable progression of courses, the concept of *mezze* is a spontaneous free-for-all, an antithesis, even a threat, to structured order. The dishes are all served and consumed at the same time in no specific rank. This communal approach is reinforced by the crossing of hands, and the exchange of sometimes more than twenty different dishes. Well, my feast has concluded, and the procession has reached its end. It is almost twenty to ten and I shall have to reunite with my Attorney friends again.

7

In the preface to his cookbook, Muhammad Hasan al-Baghadi cut pleasure into six parts. Food was the most noble and consequential of these delights. What al-Baghadi forgot to mention is that a man's eating is proportional to his deeds. I need all of the recipes compiled in his tasty tome to muster the courage to proceed. But that is not enough. I need the searing heat of a frying pan, the concentrated energy of Ghaemi's flan. I need to count the calories crowded in those fragrant pages, tarnished with coriander and caraway seeds.

As I ride to B 018, a stench more putrid than death permeates the night. It tickles my urge for a steak, causes my appetite to ache. B 018 is an industrial dance club tucked in a deserted district called The Quarantine. Christian forces stormed the area in 1976, killing hundreds and forcing many more to flee. When the war ended, an architect named Bernard Khoury built the B 018 on top of the plundered camp. Today it offers the best nightlife in the Levant. I pedal faster and faster along the city port, past the trash dump that stands out like a giant wart. And with each stroke, a whiff of rubbish, such a sweet-smelling rose, rushes into my nose.

Made of concrete and steel, B 018 is mostly underground. The street-level roof is made of mirrored panels that open to the sky, catching reflections of the city lights. Splintered portraits of a speeding car mingle with sultry scenes from the bar. The images shift in quick bursts, distracted and decadent. Above the open roof, the moon stands guard. Inside, flesh presses against glistening flesh. The roof retracts, and I catch a hazy glimmer of a dancer, pulsating between pleasure and pain. Her body curls on a mirrored panel and melts into Sadji's thin frame. How odd for him to want to meet me here, how insane.

I ponder the panorama. In the Academy, we always probe the history of a foreign city. But now that I am here, it's not quite what I expected to see. Not a single tree near the desolate dock, not even a cedar. The Bible cites the cedar more than 103 times. Each Lebanese flag has one emblazoned at its center. There must be hundreds of flags in the city, wrestling with the winds.

At the end of a deserted dock, I anchor my bicycle next to a fisherman's dory. Following a dirt road for five minutes, I find myself in front of a husky sentinel blocking off a steep stairway. He tells me that all patrons—regardless of their religious faith—must check their bags at "heaven's gate." As I unstrap my backpack, the mechanical churning of the roof scrapes the inside of my ears. I can hear clusters of flesh stomping on the cement floor, carefree crowds reeling on rainbow cocktails and beer. I stroll down the steps, pushing my way into the ecstasy. The ceiling is wide open to the sky, ready to swallow a falling bomb. Perhaps that is what all those specks are in the night: blazing bombs simulating the outlying suns.

The rancid smell of rubbish has found its way into the room, wafting in with the wind. But Beirut's brash boys don't seem to mind. They will make you believe that the handicap of the present is only a limitation of the mind. Consider this: if one believes, fundamentally, that the smell of trash is as pleasing to the nose as a purple dendrobium, who is to say that it isn't so?

Next to two eager teens, rotating on their platform heels, Sadji breaks into a swoon. He howls at the moon and the girls giggle. As he dissolves into a track by Massive Attack, I sense the pulp of Ghaemi inside me, like the wild, riotous rice, the pleasant and warm grains of basmati inside an oven-baked turkey. It would be a stunning sight to see her once more in the badlands of Beirut. She is sweeter than a thousand pralines, a cornucopia of colors that you have never seen: pigments of citron yellow and potter's pink, purple-peach, a Hyde Park green that is a grade lighter than dill. Hold still, my will. What this pastel portrait needs is a few strokes of violent vermilion like the (belated) blood that I plan to spill.

8

NOUGAT WHITE and licorice black have always been my favorite colors. The source of this discovery was an almond-eyed girl in our village. Her name was Ghaemi Basmati. When I first saw Ghaemi, it was from the saddle of my new birthday gift, that cumbersome bicycle with twelve gears to shift. She skipped and hopped across the dusty souk, lugging a basketful of fruit. It takes a lot to buckle my knees, though not on that particular day. She was a force that I had never seen. Soon after, I lost control of my handlebar. Everything around me turned a celestial white except for Ghaemi, who has the angelic color of light cocoa. By any measure (preferably metric), that was a minor bicycle accident, the first of many more to come. But it was the second most important that I have ever had. It was a collision that shuddered my world. I remember that she wrapped her scarf around my wounded knee. She apologized a thousand times. My tongue was tied in ten thousand knots. I was hopelessly hypnotized. Hobbling back to my village home, we passed a triad of shrines: a synagogue, a mosque and a church. And then we sat on the porch. We drank mint tea that Mother had made. We decided to meet the following day under Joshua's Arcade.

Ever since we met, our fates have been intertwined like grapevines. Together, we explored caves where bats had wings the size of DC-10s. I would pull on her pigtails like great knells before fighter jets flew over us. We became best friends, climbing the rugged hills of the Galilee and dipping in the warm waters of the Mediterranean Sea. We sipped warm rosewater instead of Darjeeling tea. We shared everything: our marbles and our fears. I remember courting Ghaemi past the grocers of our village souk. She led the way, and I'd pedal after her on my green bike with the dexterity of a mountain goat. With each year I became more drunk on her words, teasing me, taunting me, tossing my insides upside down. And then one day, we joined the Academy, and all of these moments were lost to a politics of division and hostility. And all the children with whom we played in the village fountain were gone. I could no longer see them. All of those portraits that I had thought were indelibly scorched into my subconscious faded away. But perhaps if you listen intently, you may hear the gurgle of Arabic and Hebrew rising from our village fountain, spraying your ears with splashes of water: how I miss that polyglot palaver.

It is my biggest wish that you have a crippling accident one day: an injury as big as the Academy. And surely you will if you have not already had the pleasure of a cracked head that has taken you to the precipice of death. (There is no proxy for practice.) Depending on the magnitude of your injury, a cosmic crash can put a dent in your fate, derail you from a seemingly predestined path, or if you prefer, put you on the path that you always willed but were unable to see; push you beyond the constraints of nationality. Just take a look at me: I am half this, half that. My favorite colors are nougat white and licorice black. And if you look closely at my skin, you will see pigments of purple, Chinese yellow, fawn brown and Bat Yam blue, my mother's favorite hue. But if the nation is dead, why are we together in the same bed? Eating from the same plate; walking hand in hand like two hungry lovers, our cheeks burning a vital and violent red.

9

THE MECHANICAL GRIND of the roof quivers my body. The mirror panels converge, sealing us inside the frenzy of B 018. I'd rather be in a canteen, eating a can of beans. All around me, an army of teens in tight vinyl and torn jeans drown their sorrows in fizzy drinks. A loud couple next to me chat in Frablish: a fusion of French, Arabic and English. "*Ya habibi,* I couldn't say *je t'aime* or *je t'adore* as I longed to do, but always remember, I'm saying it. Now give me a big *bawsi.* A historic kiss, *un grand bisou, mon petit chou.*" She reaches over to her. This is the required lingua franca spoken by the local elite, whose duty is to impress, never to oppress. Some people will never have a language this whole.

With each burst of light, I catch a glimpse of their glasses clinking; a cherry cocktail, floating. Glimmering, white teeth. Twirling his body into the music, Sadji shifts into overdrive. I have rarely seen him so alive. He's having a feast of the heart: one last ritual of joy before we serve our explosive baby boy.

I shut my eyes, and Ghaemi whispers into my ear. How true it is that if you think of angels, you hear the sound of their wings. And that whenever the name of a good person is mentioned, there she appears. "Come with me," Ghaemi says. We walk to the bar. It is the longest walk that I have ever taken, longer than a breadless day. My heart pounds, pacing the music's busy beat. I almost trip over my clumsy feet.

"Always getting into accidents," she says. "I can't believe Sadji planned our meeting at such an unfamiliar place."

"He's our Doyen of Deception, what do you expect?"

"I hope I'm wrong." She looks at me with half-comprehending eyes. "Although for the first time since the market tragedy, Sadji feels that you've become soft."

The market tragedy was the pivotal event that galvanized the forces of retaliation in the Academy. The bombing took place in the souk, the open market of my childhood village where Arabs and Jews have lived together since antiquity. The Academy believes that the Followers of Fareed planted the bomb at the center of the market. The bomb missed its intended target: a synagogue near the cave and Yasef's home, past the pots of melissa and mint.

I remember, Ghaemi and I were sitting under Joshua's Arcade, drinking lemonade that Mother had made. All of a sudden a blast bigger than Byzantium shook our tiny village. The ice in our drinks shattered together with the glass. The blast was perverse and unbearable. Uprooted by its explosive force, I belched delirium. My body lost control. My face turned yellow. In the corridors of my mind, concrete walls crumbled; my center wrecked. And for a second, everything turned a volcanic obsidian, the way things do when I am flushed with intense and fantastic pain.

Ghaemi ran to the village center in Gargantuan strides. I rode after her, trying to block off the surrounding howls. Amidst the rubble, we searched the charred bodies for familiar faces. I counted twenty-seven dead, of various firmness and form; brains splattered like cabbage; twelve dismembered limbs; four charred feet (two under the age of seven); five frangible hands. There were mangled and twisted men next to mangoes, beets and bloodstained baskets. And among the delicate, broken ankles, underneath this epidermal wreck, were Muslims, Christians and Jews: a plunder of paradox. Circling a heap of bodies, we found Ghaemi's parents, sprinkled with lentils. Beads of tears slid down my burning cheeks.

I raced on my bicycle until my legs failed. But I could not rid myself of that awful smell: the burnt epidermal cells spilled in the dust. I wanted to gather them all back again, each dispersed cell. I stared at the clock next to Bashir's bakery, which was also damaged by the blast.

That time has remained frozen in my mind ever since: a harrowing monument to the twenty-seven dead. My faith has never recovered from the tremor of that blast. To this day, whenever I visit my birthplace village, I am reminded of its tragic past.

That night we lit candles because the electricity was out. Ghaemi came over to our house and we helped Mother prepare lentil stew in honor of the dead. She washed the lentils carefully, and placed them in a clay pot. That is when I asked Mother about the lentils. She said: "Just as the lentil is round, so mourning comes to all the denizens in the world." Or perhaps it's because worries are easier to bear with lentils than without them.

Ever since the bombing in the open market, where farmers gathered once a week to sell their harvest, the Academy's ranks have swelled. And while the event occurred more than a year ago, in the Middle East, a year is an eon, the largest division of geological time; a centimeter of land can be more vital than a hectare, and every shred of memory is etched in ancient stone. In the Middle East, even the branches of the same olive tree fall in different countries.

Such deep-seated antecedents left little choice to the Academy but to retaliate. And so following the open-market bombing, our attacks and counterassaults have started to escalate. First it was simply "blood for blood, soul for soul, child for child." But now the calculus has changed. The decimals have become more damning. We are considering using multiplication signs instead. We are moving from hard targets, as Sadji likes to say, to soft ones. Just like a little honey bun. Six eyes for an eye, a dozen hands for a hand. Onward to the Summerland.

10

ON THE DANCE FLOOR, Sadji sizzles like a steak. He smiles at us as his body continues to break. There is one last thing that I need to know. I ask Ghaemi if the Academy arranged my grandfather's visit to the hospital.

"To help you recover," she says. "There is no substitute for your mother's cooking, no advice that is weightier than your grandfather's. You are lucky to have them all."

"You know, I can do without Mother's lentil stew."

"So you prefer the menu of our replacement family, the Academy?"

"We'll have our own family one day."

Surely, our baby will be the opposite of the mechanical miscreant: a momentous male with beady little eyes; lips more lush than the pink inside of a salmon; a tummy softer than a hotel pillow. And we'll coddle him, then slide him into a seat on the back rack of my bicycle and take him for a ride. We'll make him wear a helmet at all times. Make sure that it fits snugly. That the chin strap holds firmly against the throat, that the buckle is fastened securely.

"You don't have to promise me that," she says. "There is something that I have to tell you. Today spring is putting in her second appearance of the year and I'm very grateful."

"What is it?"

"Last week we had a huge drama: blood on the floor in the apartment opposite the Academy, banging on the doors, police, swish telescopes. It turned out to be pomegranate juice and not blood. So not really an anecdote worth telling, I'm afraid."

"Is that what you wanted to tell me?"

"Not really." Her smile is as wide as the Fertile Crescent. "I have a surprise for you and it's not an edible treat. It's inside me; a full-frontal surprise: a baby with a tiny nose."

Kismet, I suppose.

I fall down on my knees as if I'm about to propose. Instead, I stick my ear against Ghaemi's belly. I'm not used to this kind of sticky prose. How odd that a living cherub can grow inside her: a spoonful of my fatty cells and a dash of my dendrites; a piece of posterity whipped into one animate whole. In a few months, the baby will pleasantly float in his mother's womb. And one day he'll push his way out into a hospital. We'll coddle him, then swaddle him in a blanket. We'll give him a gentle slap on his back and he'll let out a cough. He'll whimper the way I suppose all babies do. And then he'll release an explosive cry more powerful than a bomb.

11

GHAEMI, who has studied the genealogy of bombs for many years, holds my head in her palms. To be a father so close to death makes me think of the unknown that he will enter. How odd it must be to join a world where some make war, others omelets; to be faced with a multiplicity of choices, conflicting forces, some competing for his attention, others paying little notice to him, because he is already part of a process, a tiny molecular maize in a galactic mill. Will he be refined or unrefined, astringent or mild-mannered, a slave to tradition or a partisan of transcendence? My shoulders feel light. The atlas at the northern tip of my spine is no longer shrugged. I'm flushed with a happiness lighter than helium. I press my ear into her tummy. Bursts of thunder echo inside her digestive tract. An army of barley *farfel* wages war against some other furtive snack. The round shape of the *farfel* is a symbol of fertility and the wish that our misdeeds fall away. But tomorrow is another day. Ghaemi presses her body against mine. My nose is lost inside her flesh, savoring the smell of our baby. So much converges there. One womb, a cross-current of culture. Dispersed diasporas bound together biologically. Spermatozoan circling the egg. Some are genetically encoded to have a big nose. Others are programmed to reject lactose. Is there meaning in such a lottery? All of them are fueled by the raw energy of life. Or more precisely by the desire to live. They break barriers, disperse and regroup. A few will lose their way in transit. The tougher ones will fall down and get up. Only one will survive. The rest will die like . . .

I look at the heaps of flesh around me, at the animate bodies holding on to fizzy drinks. On the dance floor, bodies linger from side to side like weary cyclists climbing a hill. At the bar, four friends are having a tiff over the bill. It's as if it were the breakup of the Balkans they were considering. So much politics can be injected into such petty things. One of them grabs the bill: "Let us talk the matter over. Not exactly the partition of Palestine. Let's not make this more complicated than it is." I prefer the Balkan analogy. It's not that I feel an intimate connection to that part of the world. But there is safety in distant places.

It's easier to accept the geography of a land we have never been to: the cozy coordinates of the Far East or the noble baobab of the Sahel. We embrace the nebulous with open arms. That's why the Punjab smells so pleasantly pungent. It is an abstraction that can be absorbed and kneaded into my imagination. The stars too were created for this purpose. Just open your arms and they are yours: from the tiniest subatomic particles to the superclusters. The quasar is our closest ally. It is hidden in the far, outer reaches of the universe. Nothing like a long-distance relationship. It is different with a neighbor. We resent them a little.

The Cyclist

The mechanical ceiling above us churns. The mirror panels open to the night, embracing the anatomy of the universe. Ghaemi stares at the moon, at the clusters of unborn suns.

"I must leave you now with your bicycle," she says. *"Yihiyeh beseder."* All will be well.

12

SADJI STRAGGLES over to the bar. He's wearing a bracelet and a fake goatee. With Sadji an image is never as it seems. A silver ring, the size of a Life Saver, hangs from his nose: he is a master of the deep-cover pose. As our Designer of Deception, he keeps our true intentions at the fraying edges of the world. He scours continents and the Academy picks up his debts. He walks across the Negev in search of bedouins, who live on the mesa. He hires them to map the vast wadis of this ancient land. They know the trail of windswept sand like the backs of their hands.

Soaked in liquor and sweat, he wraps his arms around me.

"There was a little complication with Leng," he tells me. "Having been rather nearsighted, the risks were high that he would die. Maybe I could have done something to hide his identity, to lock it tight inside a jar."

Years of soldiering are just starting to crack Sadji's once unflappable rigidity.

"The execution of this mission has been a very trying and tedious experience for me." He grips my right arm for empathy. "Not unlike baking a log of *mandelbrot.* There is always the risk that one will use too many walnuts or toss out the almonds. With Leng, I am sorry to say, the risks were higher."

"The mission, compromised?"

"Contaminated. Not compromised. I still like the vast possibilities, the huge potential, the way Fareed and his followers make you want to seize the day, and do anything and everything. So you see, in spite of our little setback, the shower party goes on. If you survive, you'll come back to the Academy. The posthumous rank of corpulent awaits you."

"If I survive?"

Sadji pulls back his jacket and I see the butt of a revolver sticking out of his waist, black as an eggplant.

"Low probability, I'm afraid. As I said, the loss of Leng has prompted a slight change in our plan. The enemy has since heightened security at the Summerland. So we want you to deliver the baby straight from your bosom. Your wound will be fatal. Try to be brave and philosophical."

"I don't understand."

"What's there not to? A man's true value comes to light the moment they say that he is dead. Perhaps someone will write about you one day. You may even get a citation in *The Little Known Tragedies of the Academy.* It's useless to resist immortality."

Unmoved by such postulates, teenagers around us drink and dance, stomp and yell, living, as they *are,* with different meanings and metaphors. I can feel the sweat burning on my pores.

"They are all softies." Sadji waves at them. "Like Rimbaud said: 'Expel from your mind all human hope, strangle it. Bite the ends of their guns as you die. Disaster shall be your God.' "

The Cyclist

A blast for a blast, six eyes for an eye, a dozen hands for a hand. Onward to the Summerland.

To gain my full sympathy, Sadji grabs my neck.

"Excuse my fervor, but long ago, I was instructed to avenge the death of a baby, one of our own," he explains. "We carried crates of explosives into the enemy village."

His voice trembles in regret, even if it is for a fleeting moment. "We blew up forty-five homes in retaliation. It was before the crack of dawn, and the village men had run off into the hills. It was dark, and I could not tell if there were women and children inside the homes. Later that day, I stretched out in mud, dried myself in criminal air, played clever tricks on my insanity so that I could protect my sanity."

And so the sun shone, the acacia tree blossomed and the slaughterer slaughtered.

"We don't want to interfere in their internal affairs," he demurs. "Once this raid is over, I'll be the first to come here as a tourist."

"What about me?"

"There is just one more item. Are you ready?"

"I need a drink."

"Take this earpiece. It's a wireless receiver that will allow us to communicate with you while you ride. It has been molded to fit comfortably inside your ear canal."

"From your mouth into my ear."

"Let's go over your itinerary. You have everything now: the baby, the backpack and the bicycle. Show up at the starting line at dawn. Try to smile as if you are a citizen of the world. Look Dutch. Unassuming, bland."

My favorite cyclist is Joop Zoetemelk, the carrot-haired Dutchman whose last name means "sweet milk." Since the age of eleven—when my parents gave me my first bicycle—I have watched videos of him compete in every international race. I would pretend that it was me winning the race. But I never could, because a glutton always keeps a slow pace.

"Remember, five minutes into the race, you must trail everyone."

Like a man with a razor stuck in his throat, if I spit it out it will be a calamity, and if I swallow it, it will be a disaster. Will I have the courage to make a stand?

"At our command, you'll break off to the Summerland."

The Ride

1

THE ROAD TO TERRORISM usually begins with a pinch of alienation; a dab of ennui. My advice to those who want to avoid this condition is to increase their intake of honey. Try it with a cup of Earl Grey to wash away the prosaic crumbs stuck in your tummy. Depending on your taste, you may prefer a gram of royal jelly: the preferred palliative of the region's monarchy. Secure in her hive, this is the honey that the queen bee feasts on. So if it's good enough for a queen, it surely is adequate for a cretin.

You must excuse me for these culinary asides. But if it's not ennui that affects one, then drill a second hole into my head. You may not like what you see there, whether a priori or in irreparable experience. You will surely lose the links between cause and effect. And that is how it should be. I'm not some Pavlovian pawn who explodes bombs every time Mother makes a meringue. My feelings are more delicate than a soufflé. So what is the good of this catharsis if you will be unable to prevent the tragedy that awaits the Summerland? Well all right, here is what the doctors have to say. Not the ones who patched up my brain, but the terrorism experts, the theoretical menders of my wounded mind.

Some of us are said to suffer from faulty vestibular functions in the middle of the ear. Or perhaps from inconsistent parenting. Fortunately, there is nothing wrong with my hearing (except for a slight case of bomb shock I suppose).

There is so much torment in terror, my father the art scholar used to say. And I have seen countless paintings documenting pain and torture in his dense, academic tomes. But not in the darkest of my dreams could I have conjured up a terror so tangible and untame. How is it that the sadistic impulses captured by a canvas, those gardens of torture and death, those etchings of axe and stake, so improbable and horrific, could spring to life from the sterile pages of his books? I wish it were your neighborhood instead. Consider those maimed and mangled corpses huddled next to you in your bed. Let the graves return the dead. What happens next? My dearest Ghaemi, I am not sure. But at least centuries ago, the bodies of hanged men were raised on wooden gallows so that they would not be devoured by dogs and wolves.

2

DURING THE SLOW and wrenching weeks that followed the market tragedy, I drifted dependently on my bicycle through the wounded streets of our village. Everywhere I looked, objects and people practiced an inverted sort of physics. When I said hello to an old woman, she did not reply. When I screamed in the arched tunnels of the souk, the echo refused to billow in my ears. I stuffed my tummy with endless servings of pastry. It all stayed inside me. I skipped my customary mint tea before going to sleep. Yet, somehow, I peed profusely during the course of the night. And then, one day, I stopped to weep. For every action, there was always some odd reaction.

One morning as I rode to the village center, I saw several men asking questions of our neighbors. One of them came up to me and introduced himself as a recruitment officer for the Academy. He was tall and thin, like the spike of a sugarcane. He had a crooked nose and his red hair flared out like a fan brush. The first question he asked was how I felt about the blast. I told him there was only one person in the entire village that I would want to see dead and that was the candy store owner next to Ghaemi's home. How I loathed the *mlabbas* he sold, the sugar-coated nuts, which he sprinkled with saccharine to save a few coins. The second question he asked explored my likes and dislikes. That was easy, I thought. I really like to ride my bicycle. I eat with a passion that is more fiery than a pinch of paprika. I am allergic to *ponchiks,* the sugar-powdered Polish fritters that Ghaemi's mother used to make. I try to avoid the *kik wot,* the fiery but heavily spiced Ethiopian veggie stew that has become more common in our holy land in recent years. The last question he asked was whether I would ever consider interviewing with the Academy. If it helped to take us closer to the perpetrators of the market tragedy, yes I would. "The only way to deal with a walnut is to crack it," he said. And then, like Noah's raven, he went away.

I suppose one can be philosophical and ask as I do every day why some of us return home safely after a morning of shopping at the fish market, sifting through rows of mollusk and marlin, while others become the target of a mugging, a beating, even a bombing. For years I have wrestled to find the answer. But what is the point of procrastination? The road to terrorism does not begin with boredom. It starts at the top of the Shouf, the wondrous and wandering mountain ranges above Beirut.

Trust me, I know these things.

3

MY DEAREST GHAEMI and our unborn baby, I will promise the two of you one thing because this time I cannot afford to make an error. I promise to wear a helmet during the ride. I will make sure that it fits snugly. That the chin strap will hold firmly against the throat. That the buckle will be fastened securely. Even so, you should realize that some brain injuries cannot be prevented with a helmet. I say this not to scare you, but to better prepare you for the unforeseen.

Not to worry. This morning all of the cars have been swept off the highway. While the race is still hours away, cyclists are conducting drills along the rugged hills of the Shouf. A French cyclist from Cannes adjusts his Ray-Bans. The Syrian riders agree not to reject the race plan. Most are medium built, legs shaved. Some of the more aged riders have bulging varicose veins.

As I look at the silver rush of spokes around me, curious villagers come out of their homes to watch the event. The spectators represent a wide cross section of faith and nationality. Some of the women are veiled. A few of the men are dressed in bloomers and cummerbunds. They stand next to visitors from all parts of the world, Riga and Riyadh, the Urals and Utrecht, Bengazi and Basel. My stomach thunders. How I wish I could nibble on a wedge of cheese and some basil. My tendons stretch with the morning call of the rooster. The tires roll over the asphalt and we pass a pond. The gears clink: a greeting of sorts to the cedars beyond. Rolling along hillocks, we climb higher and deeper into the Shouf. We weave side to side, elbow to elbow along a narrow road that leads to the start line. We roll through Dair al-Qamar and its ivory-hued stones. Perched on one side of a hill are limestone dwellings. The homes in Dair al-Qamar have green wooden shutters, many of which are open in anticipation of the race. Anonymous hands sprout from windows, waving at the riders below. Faces with fierce mustaches swing from side to side. It is these unwieldy whiskers and brazen beards that give us security in life. The beard is a fundamental accessory of the fundamentalist. Does it protect him from danger? Can it act as a shield, even a weapon, against others?

I suddenly find myself leading a procession of little boys and girls into the misty hills. I must have been the Pied Piper in another life, toting a flute instead of a bomb.

In the shadow of the pines, children chase the riders with plastic squirt guns. On one side of the paved road, a mother pursues her son. Gasping for breath, the boy runs along my side with all of his strength. As we approach the vertiginous bend of a pass, he tugs at my backpack like a pot that has found its proper lid. I tap on my breaks and stamp my feet.

"Will you have breakfast with us before the race?"

It is said that one's stomach is one's enemy. I have always considered it my best friend. "Who is the cook?" I ask. The boy's mother catches up to us, offering amends for her son's offense.

"We would be honored if you joined us. It is the dream of my son to have a bicycle one day."

The boy looks at me as if I were a miracle. Someday the baby that Ghaemi is making will look at me the same way. The glimmer in his eyes reminds me of the time when my parents gave me my first bicycle. It was a used touring bike with a rusty frame and a squeaky chainwheel. I stayed awake the entire night, spinning the spokes, adjusting the gears, a drop of oil on the derailleur, a whiff of air into the front wheel.

"We will be honored if you break bread with us. Please, will you not join us?"

But of course I will, for a meal.

4

LUGGING THE BABY on my back, we follow the aroma of wood fire in the air. "In the mountains of the Shouf there are one thousand proverbs," says the boy. "And only one pudding worth eating." The mother smiles and we continue our walk along a dirt path, the boy escorting my bicycle. Their home is perched on the highest and finest spot in Dair al-Qamar. Unlike the limestone villas below, which are chiseled with an instrument known as the *shahouta,* the roof of this one is built of tree trunks. The profound smell of poplar fills my lungs. We step inside. In the kitchen, the aromatics are so intense, they can make me commit a villainous offense.

There are pots and pans on a crowded stove. The room is flavored with spice and smoke. A puff of steam wafts into my nose. "Please sit here on the mattress," the mother says. "Make it yourself like it is your home. Have some dates. The bedouins call it 'the bread of the desert.' "

Newspapers are spread on the floor. I notice one page has an article about today's event. The headline reads: "Beirut's Biggest Bicycle Race." Another blares: "Leaders Move Ahead on Peace Process." The mother shakes her head from side to side. "Let me tell you about this process," she says. "The big men are cooking and the little people are eating. We will take what we are served."

Delectable *dibes* is placed on the paper. This is an alternative to jam, made from crushed, cooked grapes and served with sesame paste. As Middle Easterners may know, preparing preserves is a tricky task as a balance must be struck between pectin, sugar and acid. The complications are many, but preserve advocates are hopeful. It is clear that grapes are rich enough in pectin to produce lasting gels on their own. However, there are other less fortunate fruits like apricots and peaches that need a supplemental source of pectin.

My favorite preserve is the one with dates. In the book of Psalms, it is mentioned that the righteous shall flourish like a palm tree. So I spread a princely portion of the luscious preserve on a slice of bread. Then in one fell swoop, the boy attacks a clay bowl of *foūl:* the Goliath fava beans mired in garlic, lemon juice and simmering oil. This was the same dish that Sadji had devoured in the hospital under my tortured nose. Now I could eat to my heart's content.

"We never had such a big race," the boy says. "Do you think you will win?"

"That's difficult to say. There are so many of us."

"I want you to win."

5

THE FLOOR IS A MEDLEY SPREAD: purple turnips, pickled limes and hot loaves of flat, round bread. The mother, who reigns supreme in the kitchen, sits next to the water jug, waiting to obey any command. Maybe the Academy should send her to the Summerland. The boy is famished, fidgeting about like a newly caught fish. I tear a piece of bread and dip it into a lentil dish. And so the peace party begins. In the Arab world a popular lentil and rice dish that one finds in every home is the *mujaddara,* a mess of potage that has been around for more than two thousand years. It is as Lebanese as bacon and eggs are British.

As a dish, the *mujaddara* has secured a spot far beyond culinary lore. It is cited in the biblical account of Esau's great hunger. For a dish of potage, Esau sold his birthplace to his twin brother as the firstborn. This gave rise to the saying: "A hungry man would sell his soul for a dish of *mujaddara*." I suppose we all have to do some sort of soul selling somewhere along the line. Unless we can live off our existing wealth, then we have to grin and bear it and sell, whether it be luscious tarts or terror, lentils or ideals. So it seems to me that of the many vocations and schools, the Academy has not been the worst. That is, until now. I am neither the first, nor will I be the last. But I will become a dad in less than nine months, a reality that very few men would disavow.

Look close at me, inside my pores. I am not the cipher that you think I am. Who stole our youth, Ghaemi's and mine? How did the fury of violence, coincidental or designed, partisan or without purpose, tint our vision of the world? If I were next to our imminent son, I would pry into nature's logic to shield him from all that is tragic. I would top off the potholes in a city road. I would recalibrate the life-bruising odds and sway the forces of chance in his favor. The mathematics are complex, the values transcendental. I am not thinking of the mechanical miscreant which Ghaemi helped spawn: our other explosive baby boy. What I have in mind is a real infant with a knob of a nose. So I ask you, is it not shameful that as a father of an unborn child I end my life, leaving no trace of myself behind? Just a mound of rotting bones, a gutted hotel, a wilted rose. My apologies for the sweet-and-sour prose. There is a hotel I need to explode.

6

AFTER BREAKFAST, the boy sweeps barley grains from the floor. He then pulls out a silver-inlaid tray from the kitchen drawer. "Hope you are ready for the drink." Then, slowly, the mother pours a crimson liquid from a jar into three glasses. "It is only for the special occasion," says the boy. "Juice of pomegranate." The glasses are long and cold.

There are people in Eastern lands with a predilection for the pomegranate. And they tell stories of how a goblet of its juice helps to regulate their hatred. In the days following the market tragedy, it would have taken a cauldron of the crimson drink to cleanse my anger. But when pregnant with promise, an average-size glass should be enough. That is 613 of the red-and-pink seeds, to be precise, each corresponding to the number of commandments in the Torah. I look into the glass, at the hapless pieces of floating ice. I think of Sadji's advice. "Ride slowly, until you are last. Then go in the direction of the shower party. Activate the blast." How many sips would I need to take to purge these dark thoughts from my head?

"Make it yourself like it is your home," says the boy's mother. "Put your backpack on the floor."

With the baby inside, I would rather not.

"To your health. Longer than a thousand years."

"To your strength. So that you can win the race."

"To your hospitality."

Our glasses clink. If Sadji were to see me, surely he would explode in a fit of fury. I take a sip of the cool drink as liquid thoughts

stir in my head in a great big circle, slowly turning into a thick cur-
dle. How typical of me to search for solid things, the traits that un-
derpin an English pudding. There is something to be said about
consistency, the coagulation of our actions from idea to deed. During
my sojourn in the hospital, precise quantities of foreign liquids entered my body. Who knows what else they injected into me. I was a
drugged-up giant on an IV; an emaciated zucchini. I fed on my
thoughts instead of my actions. But there was one which planted itself in my wounded head like the profound and pungent stem of a
musky fungi, hidden in the dark hinterlands of my subconscious: we
should strive for inconsistency at certain times. The next time you
savor a silvery smelt or a jellied fish, break with habit. Abandon your
glass of white wine for a red. Watch your waiter's face break into a
cataclysm of stress. At first, you may suffer from gastrointestinal dis-
tress. But the joy that will ride into your trite and tired tongue will
slowly settle on your palate. You must think that I'm a bit deranged,
though I am starting to acquire a taste for change.

7

BEFORE I START my ride to hell, it's time to say farewell.

"You are the most welcome. Please come again."

Running circles around me, the boy asks if he could show me the
way back to the paved road. I resist giving him a tender hug (protocol requires that I remain smug). I help him mount my bicycle instead. We pass bramble and bush toward Dair al-Qamar. Along the

ribbon of mountains, I can see the riders are already gliding down a winding road toward the hotels below. They disintegrate into a curve as if blown apart by a bomb. Moments later, they reappear, this time broken into smaller knots. The race has begun and I seem to have lost precious time.

"It's time to say good-bye," I tell the boy, helping him off the bicycle. He forms the patent *V* sign with his two hands. I have seen this emblem flashed by both vanquished and victor. It is more familiar than the national currency, more commonplace than a chickpea.

"I hope you win, mister. God willing, you will."

I mount the bicycle and attack the spiral logic of the highway, the cement artery that leads to the sprawling city below. My path is clear. My tummy is no longer hollow. My hands are mammoth again. My body is no longer in pain. I can lift a mamluk with his shackles. I can roll boulders up the Hill of Shouts while puffing a Noblesse (just don't tell the Academy, please).

The Romans invented the first roads. But the most wicked of asphalt roads stretches from the highlands (some would say the badlands) of Barouk to the Beirut coast. It is peppered with impressive guards that the Academy calls the Kalashnikov Boys. They come from the deepest Lebanon: tawny teens in khaki green, sinewy soldiers looking somber. But can they see through my committed calm? Can they stop the bicycle bomber?

8

RIDING IN FIXED GEAR, I fit the wireless receiver into my ear. My cleated soles are clipped to the metal, channeling all of my power into the thrust of the pedal. Gaining my stride, I shift into a higher gear, swallowing more asphalt with each turn of the pedal. I am escaping death. I have fled its hold from a hospital bed and if I try hard, surely, I can do it again. But it pursues me, demanding attention, anxious to convey a special status to those who are in danger. I rocket to the front, passing three riders. They look resigned, half spent. One of them crashes into a tree during a steep descent. With each revolution, I hurtle closer to our unborn baby. Each twitch of my muscle is the exuberance of life, a jolt to my sensory order. Will I ever consider a tart pie, an American apple turnover?

If I place an extreme value on consumption, it's to keep my tongue open to sensation. There is a culinary shibboleth that I have always adhered to: try a bit of this and a bit of that. Avoid dishes that are difficult to make, nothing too rococo. Aim for regional equality. And so, barring a few biased responses to untenable tastes, I crave the *krepish* as much as the *kunafa*. The *krepish* is a Yiddish pastry that Mother used to make. The fillings of cabbage and kasha are a sensory tease. The *kunafa* is an Arabic sweet made of shredded wheat and cheese. There is another tenet that guides my consumption. It is the idea that opposites unite or that the quality of one sensation shall complete the other (and I'm not just thinking about sweet-and-sour soup). Without an adversary, the world would be static. Without death, life too would lose its logic. There would be no fear, no enemy to resist. I clench my fists, throwing my thrust into the mechanical beast, sprinting without patience, away from the hotel lobby, the sacrificial frenzy that awaits me. All around me, an eerie silence.

9

LIKE A RACE AROUND THE PARK, my thoughts swirl in circles. The tires roll over the road. My thighs pump the pedals hard. The gears clink, a greeting of sorts to the cedars beyond; a quiet nod, a nudge, a grunt. Struggling on my wheel, I try to avoid the hurdles along my way: potholes, sewer grates, dust and debris. Suddenly, just as I roll over a gentle ramp, the Academy sends a travel advisory. The wireless device vibrates in my ear. It's Sadji trying to undermine my measured progression of velocity.

"Slow down. Redirect the baby to the hotel lobby."

Sweeping down a series of rocky bends, I overtake seven riders.

"Slow down I said."

His message has heft: if the enemy is killed, could the meaning of my destruction be fulfilled in the act itself?

"Don't you remember how you trailed my lead while I completed five loops around Hampstead Heath? Have you forgotten the bread we shared?"

It is said that when you feed people, you buy their loyalty. Of course that depends on the kind of food that is being served. For Sadji food meant conquest and not consumption—conquest over the hearts and loyalty of other men. For me eating always brought with it death, even if it was in its accidental form: a roasted chicken, a braised fish, a rosy steak or some other dish. From the cockles of my heart, I want to defy the Academy's wish: to ride my bicycle into death's own belly. The baby's consequences are decisive. Its reach is deadly. Its encroaching force is sufficient to secure the headlines in tomorrow's paper: "Suicide Bomber Rocks the Summerland." But tastes change over time. Even a sugar-coated plum can cloy when piled on.

Sadji continues to chide me gently. "Tap your breaks. Slow down. Think of the baby on your back." Clinging to the hills, the riders fall behind in singles and pairs. I add to my pace, swishing around a hairpin bend. There is little time to make amends. I should be thinking of my other baby, the humanity of its pink and plump flesh.

"Slow down I said or I shall have to join the race." Another warning, another rider. Each admonition releases a steady flow of excess force into my muscles, bordering on explosion. Each call to duty implies an advantage, not for me but for the coming of the new-born.

I cruise next to a rider called Abu Khalid, who has earned the nom de guerre "the Cannibal" for turning his rivals into mincemeat. I follow his lead, unable to mount an effective attack. The baby is still attached to my steely back. The chase continues for fifteen minutes along curvy slopes and narrow roads. We plunge along the mountain, passing pines, sweeping down the last series of bends into the city. Abu Khalid shifts to an infernal pace in the direction of the coastal highway, having built a lead of at least five minutes over the nearest pack of cyclists. They will need a miracle to win the race. Somehow, I manage to follow the leader's pace. As we approach the coast, I spot the banked angle of a wayward rider swaying from side to side. It's Sadji speaking into a tiny phone. His bike has a bell, a temperamental three-gear system and squeaky brakes that work in part: not a very auspicious start.

"Slow down," his voice echoes in my ear. "You're clearly not fit to carry on. The hotel is in the other part of town."

Sending another spurt of force into the thrust of the pedal, I rocket off to the lead, pressing closer to the finish line. Could victory be mine? As I ponder the question, my bicycle is shaken by a heady blast. All along the coast, crowds break into a deafening chant, waving the victory sign. Shia women in *shadors* sprinkle the highway with rose petals and rice. Others dressed in green and purple veils start ululating. Whose wedding is it that they're celebrating? On the roof of a rusty Benz, a young man sprays automatic gunfire in the air. A procession of Kalashnikov kids follow my lead. The old men pack away their worry beads. From a loudspeaker of a nearby mosque an imam hails: "After every difficulty in life there is a joyous moment of release and then a new beginning. When an uprising ends, it's time to celebrate spring." It's not just the turbaned clerics who have been infected by the merry mood. Route-side spectators, who have come from the far edges of the globe, have begun to dance the *dabka* jig, delighting in what seems to me a mystery: a riddle of a revelry.

10

OVERTAKEN BY THESE FESTIVE EVENTS, I lose my stride. The Cannibal catapults ahead of me during a high-speed romp. The

The Cyclist

Academy has taught us that to secure our existence we must learn to turn off certain stimuli. But the mayhem around me is big and loud. It's as if the shower party has spilled into the streets. The entire city is drunk on its feet. The crowd swells into a storm, driven by a collective urge. Random images fly past me, wild mobs lost in efferent fits, absent of any purposive conduct. Is it my attention that they want to abduct? There must be a reason for the celebration.

I throw my muscles into the bicycle. My posture and movement regain their rhythmic union with its metal frame. We are one and the same. As we roll over a gentle ramp, the transmitter vibrates in my ear. This time it's not Sadji but the explosive cry of a baby that I hear. My mind wanders into the tempting geography that is Ghaemi's belly.

We dart through a stormy mob, waving diverse flags. They are adorned with emblems: stars and stripes, crosses and crescents, a visual shorthand of our differences. Putting aside their fealty, a number of spectators trade rival flags. Nothing like a bit of bravura to break the ice. Surely, if they knew about the baby and the dislocation that it's designed to cause, this dizzy outpouring would be lost. With each revolution, I try to escape their unruly effervescence. It's a difficult task, as the party acquires the dimensions of a carnival. I maintain my gear, unable to snatch the lead from the Cannibal. Seconds later, the Academy transmits a familiar voice into my ear. It's Ghaemi, my delectable dear.

"Steer clear of trouble," she tells me. "There is a lot of confusion on the coast. Avoid the rowdy revelers. The foreign ministry just issued details of a new framework to deal with our neighbors. The news has sparked a fit of frenzy in the region's capitals."

Call me a cynic. But the first thought that crosses my mind is that our communications are compromised. If the forces opposed to the Academy are laying a trap, it would not be the first. Do you know how cavemen hunted for food centuries ago? They dug great big holes in the ground, bigger than their quarry, and then camouflaged them with branches and moss. And so the mammoth fell unwarned to its fate. One minute strong and free, the next trapped and afraid. My profession is full of elephant traps. I ride and then fall into a hole. The sides are steep and slippery. (This is not meant as a foreshadowing to a tragedy.) Thanks to the Academy, I'm well versed in the art of deception. I'm certain that it's Ghaemi's voice trying to steer me in the right direction.

"The Academy wants us to disengage," she says. "We are aborting the operation in the name of . . . Well, let me just read you the ministry's statement: 'There is a time for war and a time for peace. We have no illusions about the risks ahead. But we want to be partners in the making of peace, a peace of the brave.' "

Such is politics in the Middle East. It can turn on a shekel. Or could it be that the two sides are simply drained and no longer want to fight? Could that explain the unflagging tumult that is all around me? One must live a century of torment before reaching a peace settlement; one must demolish the human body over and over again until it is fully spent; one must puke violence in its many forms with all of its messy but honest worms. Perhaps it is only after eating the enemy's children and after they have eaten yours that nations can make peace again. The hotel today is full of tubby kids milling around: pregnant mothers pushing strollers, bundles of toddlers without a trace of hate, waiting patiently for their fate.

My thoughts spin in circles, dodging ominous hurdles. If truth be told, I am as fond of a circle as I am of a straight line. When I see a circle, I want to iron it straight and when I see a line, I want to bend it into another shape. It is no different than having to choose between a plate of fried eggplant or a bowl of gefilte fish broth. I would feel equally comfortable eating both.

"Get rid of the bomb," Ghaemi says.

In an instant my mind projects twenty years ahead. Our baby boy has grown into a young man, a soldier full of desire and at the prime of his health. I see a phantom image of him running across the magnificent future of progress, strewn with the splendor of death: curled corpses burning in flames, dismembered bodies next to instruments of war, the cadaver of a gutted tank mired in the Sinai sand. I try to imagine his eyes and when I look closely at them I see two gaping bazooka holes disguised as eyes: the same look of death in both of our eyes; the same smell of lentil stew and blood-mottled flesh grilled in the desert sand. His image flickers like an uncertain ghost, skipping and hopping over several more bodies of various firmness and form: twelve dismembered limbs, five mutilated hands that could make an assassin squirm.

Like the lean wheel of a race bike my thoughts accelerate. Neoprene wheels turn in my head as I inch closer to the Cannibal. They vary in size and make: tough tractor tires, sturdy rollers, little wheels at the bottom of baby strollers. I loosen the straps on my shoulders. My eyes burn wild. No ideal or cause is more precious than the life of a child. I dump the bomb, the dead weight of the backpack that has kept me behind the Cannibal. Without a fuse it will have no use. The backpack tumbles along the road harmlessly. A dog trots next to it only to walk away unmoved. There, at the edge of the road, is a residual vestige of our feud. Free of my existential albatross, I catapult ahead of the Cannibal.

"Let's head back home," Ghaemi says. Anxious to see our baby's face, I add to my pace, devouring bigger chunks of the road ahead. On one side of the highway, I spot a street merchant selling sweet bread. Just concentrate, sink into the bicycle and the road. It's easy, just like cooking hard-boiled eggs. All you need to do is to put them in and then after a while take them out. If only victory was as simple as that.

11

As I GLIDE to the finish line, the crowd roars, feeding my limbs with immense power. It's an outpouring that is more urgent than a bomb and it prods my sore tendons to fight on. The seconds tick. A spectator yells, sending a spoonful of energy into my body, setting off an explosion. If my duty is to escape the collective horror of a carnage, I must sprint as much with the arms as with the legs. There is a progression of purpose to my kinetic motion. A certain process is in place, some would say historic, in spite of the crowd's disjointed commotion, the wild flux that follows a sudden reversal. It is the truth of that movement where one sees the start of new life and new ways of living. I'm thinking specifically of a pudgy infant with beady little eyes; lips more lush than the pink inside of a salmon; a tummy softer than the heart of an artichoke. And I'll coddle him, then mount him on the back rack of my bike and take him on a stroll. I will make him wear a helmet at all times. Make sure that it fits snugly; that the chin strap holds firmly against the throat; that the buckle is fastened securely.

The coastal wind blows in my direction, lifting me to the end. I look back and there is the Cannibal, swinging from side to side on his bicycle. And then out of nowhere, like a useless gate that stands by itself in the middle of the desert, a parked car sends me into the cement. I'm not sure of the model or make, but I feel as though I'm in a public stadium, completely naked. The bystanders watch as if witnessing an execution. My bicycle trembles and the crowd roars in anticipation. I have difficulty recalling the moment of impact, except that the force sent me tumbling to the ground. In an instant, the world turns prune black, shriveled at the edges. I slowly lose my appetite. My senses start to fade. My blood, sweeter than a pomegranate, drains from within me. My limbs taken from me so that others can eat.

The millstones rumble when the wheat is ground.

Notes and Acknowledgments

While many of the locations in this book—such as the mountains of Barouk—exist, it is important to note that this story is fiction and that the portraits of the characters who appear in it may not be based on actual figures. Many books were important to me in my research. *On Food and Cooking* by Harold McGee was especially useful in describing the chemical process of cooking and the genealogy of the apricot. I would like to thank the New York Public Library for letting me review archival material on Near Eastern proverbs and to glean from Fouad el-Khoury's archeology research papers on the evolution of architecture in the Bekáa valley. I have drawn from a March 8, 1992, *Washington Post* article by David Ignatius; a July 9, 2000, *New York Times* article by Deborah Sontag; and transcripts of a September 10, 1989, C-SPAN interview with Thomas Friedman. The section called "Preachers in the Park" draws from a military manual introduced by the prosecution in the 2001 trial of the U.S. Embassy bombing in Nairobi. I have quoted directly from the poets Yehuda Amichai, Arthur Rimbaud and Haim Nahman Bialik, and in some cases I have reconstructed the verse.

Grateful acknowledgment is made to Roger Lowenstein, and a special thanks to Sheikh Fadel Nasser ad-Din in Daliat al-Carmel. Melanie Jackson, my agent; Geoff Kloske, my editor; Laura Clarke in Berlin. Dana Sajdi, Mara Von Sellheim, Jason Maloney, Ilham Makdisi, Jayanti Minchu in Kabul, Victor Kremer, Sarah Leah Whitson and Erlen X. Helgasdottir in Beirut. Finally, a palindromical thank you to Ara and Asa for helping me to look at the world from more than one side.

About the Author

Viken Berberian lives in New York City. This is his first novel.

Printed in the United States
By Bookmasters